nobody

ever

gets

lost

STORIES

JESS ROW

5c
FIVECHAPTERS
BOOKS

Library of Congress Cataloging-in-Publication Data
Row, Jess
Nobody Ever Gets Lost: Stories / by Jess Row.—1st ed.
p.   cm.
ISBN 978-0-982-93922-2

Book interior design by Michael Fusco

Manufactured in the United States of America
Published February 2011
First Printing

For Sonya, Mina, and Asa

Contents

So the past rots in the future—
A terrible festival of dead leaves.
—Anna Akhmatova, "Poem Without a Hero"

My body has grown cold like the stripped fields;
now there is only my mind, cautious and wary,
with the sense that it is being tested.
—Louise Glück, "October"

The World in Flames

S he first saw him sitting alone on a bench in the waiting hall of Hualamphong train station—a slight, sharp-faced white man, bending over to scratch his ankle above the sandal strap. Something about that movement was like a draft of cool dry air across her face. He wore a white linen shirt and had a haircut and was reading a magazine, paying no attention to the blaring loudspeaker, the smell of mango peels and incense and cigarettes, the barefoot farmers squatting on the floor. It was as if he came there every morning, as if it was Hampstead Heath. She sat down two seats away, put her pack between them, and began thumbing through her Lonely Planet guide, which everyone had warned her never to do in Bangkok: *make a decision about where you're going in advance and then get a taxi and go straight there and don't listen to the men who come up to you in the train station and for god's sake don't go with them.* Any sign of hesitation, any stopping to get your bearings, was an invitation. She'd thought she would go where everyone else in her train car was headed, to Khao San Road, the backpacker's ghetto, but at the sight of this man all desire for cold Heineken and fish and chips went out of her, and she had to linger, to sit down.

[margin annotations: "specific, lyrical, lucid", "mystery", "?,", "stranger in a savage land", "desire - following instinct"]

And at that moment his cell phone rang. *Wai,* she heard him say in greeting, but the rest of the conversation was drowned out by the roar of a train arriving at the nearest platform. *Missed your chance again,* she thought, *should have spoken sooner.* He snapped the phone shut, paused, and looked down at her.

That's an old guidebook, he said, in an American accent, flat, slightly nasal, at once solicitous and cold. A CNN accent. You should be careful. Half the places in there are gone by now.

second warning

I lost mine, she said, lifting her head and shading her eyes; he stood right underneath a bilious yellow-white overhead light. Someone gave me this one in Nong Khai. Better than nothing, I guess.

He took the book out of her hands and turned it to the map in the front. Baglamphu, he said, pointing to a highlighted square next to the river. Khao San Road. That's where you'll want to go. All the cheap guesthouses are there.

Actually I'm in a bit of a crisis, she said, crisply. The lie came welling up all at once, fully formed; she found herself speaking in complete sentences, outrageous and perfectly innocent. My wallet was stolen in Vientiane. And my traveler's checks. All I've got is two hundred baht that was in my pocket. I was just about to call Visa to see if they could wire me a new card.

That'll take days, he said. You shouldn't have come down here. You don't know anyone in Bangkok? This isn't a place to be hanging around with no money.

He looked at her skeptically. Her fancy red-and-black backpack, her Israeli custom-made sandals, her peasant blouse, not nearly as stained and wrinkled as it should have been, but also, she thought, her blonde curly hair, falling out of its bun, her smooth legs, relatively unscathed after two months of hard travel, turned the color of dark honey from the sun. Finally he shook his head, as if surrendering, not entirely unhappily, to the inevitable, and said, We have an extra room. My wife's just gone upcountry. You're welcome to stay overnight, if you want to.

That's very kind, she said. Would it be too awkward? I don't want to intrude.

In the taxi he spoke to the driver in Thai, leaning over the back seat and directing him across broad avenues and down alleyways crowded with pedestrians and hand-carts and noisy tuk-tuks. Every so often she glimpsed a blue-tinted skyscraper or the roof of an enormous wat, a temple, the color and shape of flames licking the sky, or some kind of white government palace, set back from the road behind a lawn and a high gate, guarded by soldiers. But mostly they travelled through a labyrinth of dark back streets that seemed never to end, one indistinguishable from the other. Bangkok was dirty, sprawling, congested, all the things the guidebook said, but she'd expected it to be more *different* from Manchester or Birmingham— not just another city full of motorcycle repair shops and dingy convenience stores and adverts everywhere for Pepsi and Britney Spears and Kool, which she could recognize instantly, even if the writing was Thai. The endless bobbing and weaving through the traffic was making her queasy.

good details

When they finally stopped he shouldered her bag and led her past a stand selling satay skewers and underneath a giant fern that made a kind of doorway leading away from the street. She saw a sidewalk, shaded and overhung with plants in containers of every kind—a jade plant in a stone box, a row of hibiscus in Chinese porcelain jars—and beside the plants, a ledge overlooking a narrow canal of gray-green water that sloshed from side to side. An old woman sat there on a plastic stool, dicing green beans onto a sheet of newspaper. The sounds of the street were entirely blotted out. He turned so suddenly she might have thought he had disappeared, and then she found herself climbing three flights of dark stairs and entering a high-ceilinged room, so sparely and quietly furnished it could have been a catalogue advertisement: *Southeast Asian Style*. Low couches in burgundy and amber prints; Lao silk hangings on carved wooden frames. The only discordant note was the computer table at the far end, and the expensive-looking office chair, all handles and curving supports. The desk was piled with papers and books, and the computer screen was lit, as if he'd walked away from it only a few minutes before.

I'm sorry, she said. I don't mean to keep you from your work. You won't know I'm here.

That's all right. He took a remote control from its wall bracket, switched on the air conditioner, and moved around the room, shutting the windows. As hot as it was, she wished he hadn't: she disliked the silent chill of air-conditioned rooms.

There's a shower in there, he said, indicating a doorway with a nod. Feel free to use it. Make yourself at home.

I haven't even introduced myself, she said. For the first time it struck her as odd that they'd been practically shoulder to shoulder for an hour and a half, and still she knew nothing whatsoever about him. It was a habit of traveling, this easy, instant comradeship—assuming that any white face in Kucha or Luang Prabang or Tiger Leaping Gorge was a fellow wanderer, someone who understood, who meant you no harm. Here they were in a city, halfway back to the First World; it wasn't appropriate. And, of course, she reminded herself, you were the one who told a lie. Out of pure instinctive desperation: for a shower, a clean floor, maybe even a drink with ice in it. Not sex per se; sex on fresh sheets, on a bed big enough to swing your legs out. All this deception was *very* much against the Backpacker's Code.

Well, to hell with it, she thought. It's just for a night.

I'm Samantha, she said, stretching out her hand. I'm from the U.K. Birmingham. Everyone calls me Sam.

Lloyd Foster, he said, shaking it lightly.

Are you American?

Canadian. But I teach in the States.

What do you teach?

Anthropology.

So you must be on leave, she said, writing a book, right?

His mouth tried to form a smile, stretching and shrinking.

My dad's a professor, she said. Economics. He was always getting leave or a grant to go off and study something someplace. India, South Africa, Brazil. Particularly when we were in our awkward stages. I think he tried to spend my entire adolescence overseas.

So you must have done a lot of traveling.

Not really. There was hardly ever enough money to go with. That's why I'm on the road now. My last best chance to see the world.

Before what?

I beg your pardon?

You said *your last best chance.*

Before I have a real job and rent to pay, and a family. The end of my prolonged adolescence. Her tinkling laugh died away as soon as it began. His eyes reminded her of tiny lenses, giving off little glints as they focused and refocused on her face. I'm actually kind of a homebody, she said. I never imagined myself as a world traveller. That was part of the idea. Testing myself. It sounds a bit New Age-y, I suppose. Like a vision quest, or a walkabout. Only the bourgeous version.

And do you have a destination in mind?

Not really, she said. I meet people and they tell me where they've been, or I read up in the book and see what looks interesting. It's not difficult. You get over the feeling of being a pinball. It's nice, actually, never having to worry if a train is late or if the bus doesn't come for three more days. You might call it a principle of karma. There's a logic behind every move, even if you don't realize it at first. She swallowed hard. Saying it to him, here, her voice ringing out in the silent apartment, it didn't sound as smart as she'd expected. So there's a reason why I lost my wallet, she said. And a reason why I met you. We'll just have to find out what it is.

Yes, he said, and though she expected him to smile, he didn't. Good, he said. We'll have to.

Only after she'd stepped out of the shower did she notice the cross hanging from a nail on the wall next to the mirror. It was perhaps four inches long, cut—or hammered, she thought—out of some kind of rusted metal. Not the kind of cross you'd expect to see in a home like this, or anyone's home; it looked like a battered artifact just dug out of the ground. Probably it was here when they arried, she thought, and they never bothered trying to detach it. She moved it to one side with a finger: the rust had stained an outline of the cross the color of dried blood into the concrete.

Religion — God — disappearing

nice

He had shown her the guest room, with its own door into the bathroom: a small room with a single high window that opened onto an airshaft. It was lined with bookshelves on three walls and had a twin bed pushed against the fourth. When she had dried herself she let the towels fall to the floor and unzipped the top of her backpack, enjoying the unexpected pleasure of nakedness. After months of scrubbing herself underneath sarongs and worming around inside her sleeping bag to change clothes it was wonderful to be in a room of her own, a room with doors she could lock if she wanted to. She'd always thought that privacy was overrated as a virtue, that the English were just obsessed with it, with their tiny walled-in backyards and separate rooms for every child. India had cured her of that idea.

Needs, she thought, I have needs like anyone else. That justifies it.

ideals v. reality

When he knocked ten minutes later she was just pulling on her last clean shirt, a tank-top she'd left in the bottom of her bag for just such an occasion. Come in, she called. He took one step into the room and stopped, still holding the doorknob, and again she felt his eyes clicking at her like shutters. She'd spread her clothes out on the bed in neat piles—bras, under-wear, shorts, t-shirts, skirts, a few printed Indian blouses and a *salwar kameez*—and now wished she hadn't, watching him take it all in with a glance.

You have a beautiful place here, she said. I didn't imagine people could live like this in Bangkok. It's incredibly quiet for being in the middle of the city.

It's a good place to work, he said. No one bothers you here. We've managed to get a lot done this year.

Is your wife also a professor?

No, no. She works for a social service agency.

You mean like an NGO?

A religious agency. A missionary group.

He's watching to see how I'll react, she thought, and in confusion, all she could think to do was laugh. I should have known, she said. There aren't so many good Samaritans in this world, are there?

Are you? he asked. Christian, I mean?

Not exactly. I was baptised—we all were, my brothers and sisters and me. But I've never been a churchgoer. She tried to make her voice neutral, factual, unapologetic. It didn't quite work. I've nothing against it, though. I'm not an atheist. Just a non-participant.

Don't worry. He gave her a faint smile, and raised his hand, palm forward, as if to stop her. You don't have to apologize. I don't blame you.

Well, you're a strange sort of missionary then, aren't you. She smiled, to show she was joking. Aren't you supposed to try to convert everyone you meet?

It isn't easy being a Christian, he said, softly. I think—we think—that it's better that you either take it seriously or not do it at all.

How elitist of you, she thought. How perfectly un-American. So I take it that's your cross in the bathroom, she said. I was wondering where that might have come from.

It's from a little village on the Burmese border, he said. It's made of hammered sheet metal they cut from a helicopter.

A helicopter?

An Army helicopter.

She'd always seen herself as a fairly good interpreter of men, their attitudes and postures and elaborately disguised emotional agendas, but here, she thought, these waters just get deeper and stranger. It was impossible to say whether his caginess was an attempt to be dramatic or a way of trying to spare her an awful truth. I'm sorry, she said, but I have no idea at all what you're talking about. Should I?

He let go of the doorknob and crossed his arms, as if unsure of what else to do with them. No, he said. I'm sorry. It doesn't matter. The point is, it was a gift. A very precious gift. Though I'll admit it doesn't look like much.

He's shy, she told herself. It's awkward, having me here. He's not used to talking to strange British girls. She had a sudden desire to flatter him, to put him at ease. I'm fascinated by Burma, she said. I'm thinking of going there next. I'd like to know more about your work.

He smiled and shook his head.

You don't, really. But it's nice of you to say so.

Come on, she said. Give me some credit. I'm not as close-minded as all that.

His eyes went up to the ceiling and stared so intensely that she had to resist the urge to turn and look at what he was seeing. You're a tourist, he said. Why would you want to hear about these things? It isn't a matter for idle curiosity. Why should you burden yourself? You don't want to know what's really going on in this world.

Sanctimonious fucker, she could hear herself saying. Imagining they were in a pub in Islington, or on the beach in Penang, for that matter. *Keep your burden if it means that much to you.* She crossed her arms and took a step back, involuntarily, nearly falling over her sandals. What is it about these people, she wondered, who think that if you don't have a position you don't have a mind at all? Her own brothers, for example: one a director of the Hare Krishna temple in King's Cross and the other a Lacanian psychoanalyst. They couldn't be in the same room, let alone sit down for dinner together; given the chance they would dispute the subtext of *Hello* or the implications of *Nice weather today.* Try me, she almost wanted to say to him, sarcastically. Test me. But before she could do anything he held up his hand again.

I'm sorry, he said. I shouldn't have put it that way. I'd be happy to explain it to you over dinner. Would you like that? We can leave in an hour or so.

She swallowed; her tongue and throat were suddenly dry

and sandpapery. That's an interesting lead-up to an invitation, she said, trying to smile again. Of course. You're too kind.

While he showered she took her journal and sat on one of the couches in the living room, instinctively tucking her legs under her in the position a guesthouse owner had shown her in Laos—so as not to offend anyone by inadvertently exposing the soles of her feet. The coffeetable in front of her was glass with a shelf underneath, piled with books: *A Political History of Southeast Asia. Barrett's Pocket Concordance. The Expatriate's Guide to Bangkok.* She picked up the guide, and saw underneath it a smaller book, supermarket-paperback sized, with a plain cover, white letters against a green background. *The World in Flames. By Walter Maddox, M.A., J.D., Ph.D.*

To the Reader, read the title of the first page.

This book assumes that you are familiar, with the Book of the Revelation of Jesus Christ and the writings of our Fathers in the Church of Jesus Christ in Rapture. If you are not so familiar, this book will be of no use to you and you should 1) put it aside until you have read the aforementioned works or 2) dispose of it immediately.

The purpose of this book is to outline the practical steps that must be taken in the next three to five years to assist the final events preceding the Day of Glory. They are strictly in accordance with the prophecies given by our Lord in the Book of the Revelation of Jesus Christ.

She turned the pages and stopped at a chapter heading: *Breaking of the Seals 1-4.*

Rev. 6:8: "They were given authority over a quarter of the earth, to kill by the sword, by famine, by plague and through wild beasts." Not-

withstanding the corresponding verse Ezk. 14:21, it is not certain that the horsemen will appear in the Holy Land. Recent observations and World Events indicate to experts that Africa may be the most likely site of the Appearance.

She turned the pages again and stopped at a diagram: *Possible readings of the seal of God on the foreheads of the 144,000.* There were six line drawings of the same smiling face: a black woman's face, with a broad nose and thick, exaggerated lips. On each her forehead bore a slightly different mark: a word in Hebrew, she thought, or Aramaic, or Greek. At the bottom of the page, printed in block letters:

REMEMBER, THE CHOSEN MAY NOT BE WHO YOU THINK!

They left the apartment at dusk, the sky turning a yellow-green color that reminded her of moldy lemons. This time a small Toyota van was waiting for them at the curb; he opened the sliding rear door for her, and then sat next to the driver, a short Thai man who wore a polo shirt unbuttoned, a wide gold chain underneath. No one spoke. It seemed to her that they were headed into the center of the city: they turned onto a broad avenue lined with hotels and shopping malls and restaurants, and passed an enormous fountain lit with red and pink and orange lights, like a giant frothing wedding cake, underneath a billboard-sized picture of the King. You saw his picture everywhere, it seemed to her: a slender, balding man with oversized square glasses, who was always looking off to the side, as if embarrassed to be there.

We've been working with a group called the Miwa, he said to her, over his shoulder, as if they had been in the middle of a conversation. It's a very small tribe—only about three thousand members or so. They live up in Chiang Rai province, right on the border, up between Burma and China. It's an undeveloped area, full of smugglers and such, and there's an insurrection going on just south of them, in the Shan State. No aid group has ever reached them before, let alone the government. And they need everything—wells, clean toilets, a health clinic. Right now I've been working with some recordings to see if I can develop a basic Miwa grammar for our aid workers. They don't have a written language, and no linguist has ever studied them before. It's all uncharted ground.

That sounds like an expensive project, she said. Where do you get the money?

Churches, he said. Our American churches, primarily. They've been very generous.

The driver slowed and darted left across a narrow gap in the opposing traffic. She put her hand against the window to steady herself, and stared for a moment at the tiny yellow eyes of the scooters flying toward her, her sphincter bunching up like a fist.

It's easy to misunderstand the kind of work we do, he said, looking straight ahead. People say that it's manipulative, that it's blackmail. As if we went into these areas and said, *we'll only help you if you become Christians like us.* It's much more complicated than that. What these people need more than anything is some good news. He turned and gave her a half-smile. How would you feel, he said, if you knew that your culture, your whole way of life, was a dead end? Your population's dwindling, you're being attacked on all sides and you don't understand why. All the animals you used to hunt have disappeared. These people *need* to hear that there's a different way.

And besides, she said, there's the question of the 144,000, isn't there?

He blinked, repeatedly, his eyelids fluttering.

I was looking at one of your books, she said. *The World in Flames.* Is that all right?

It's fine, he said, too quickly. I'm just a little surprised. I thought you weren't interested.

Do you really believe all those things? she asked. The four horsemen, and the marks on the foreheads, and the trumpets, and the War in Heaven?

He laughed. Look around you, he said. The street was jammed solid with cars and lorries, bicycles and racheting motorbikes dodging among them; the sidewalks filled with women carrying groceries and babies, stone-faced monks in bright orange robes, street vendors with enormous loads of durians and mangos slung over their shoulders. How can you think anything different? he said. Do you know what rich Thai men like to do these days? They buy twenty child prostitutes at a time and bring them home as a harem. Then, when they're finished with them, they buy twenty more. Disposable children. It's the most successful industry in the city.

But the whole world isn't Bangkok. It's a particular situation.

And what makes you so sure of that?

She remembered, in Bombay, hearing the stories of children whose parents cut off their arms and legs, or squeezed

them into boxes to deform them, to make them better beg- *good God.*
gars; mothers who rubbed hot peppers on their babies' anuses
to keep them crying until they died of dehydration. All those
hours of trying to tease out an explanation—poverty caused
by overpopulation, the breakdown of traditional rural life, cycles of abuse and neglect, the psychological effects of chronic
malnutrition—what good did it do, in the end, when their tiny
dirty hands tugged at her skirt and waved in her face? It was
arbitrary, in a way, wasn't it, this business of explaining the
world in facts and graphs and studies: an indulgence. What
was wrong with accepting such an obvious, time-honored explanation? Her grandparents had been Calvinists; this was another variety of the same concept, wasn't it?

I have to say I admire you, he said. I don't know what it
would be like to live in this world and not feel the end coming. People think it's hard for us, but how hard is it, really? To
me the real nightmare would be not knowing what's going to
happen.

The air in the van—the mingled smells of vinyl seats and
cigarette smoke, the weak A/C—was making her thick-head-
ed and sleepy. She rested her head against the back of the seat
and tried a few deep, cleansing breaths. The problem with
the analogy was that in those days everybody was a Calvin-
ist, or Catholic, or Church of England. On the same playing
field, if not quite the same team. It's different when it's you
against the world. How do you live, day by day, with that kind
of contempt, with so much revulsion, the secret of your own
superiority?

Either he's a faker or a saint, she thought. Or a fanatic of some kind. They had those in America—the ones who snuck up on abortion doctors and shot them through the window at breakfast. But that kind of thing would never happen here. And anyway he didn't have the steel for it. You could tell that instantly. This was a man who believed in decency and trusted God to dole out the punishments.

Just then he did something utterly extraordinary and un-expected: he turned and reached an arm between the front seats, grazing her bare thigh, and squeezed her hand. It was the first human touch, the first skin-to-skin contact, she'd had in weeks, since those few fumbling kisses with the Australian boy in Luang Prabang. It stirred her.

You're not trying to convert me, she said, the same way you're not trying to convert the Miwa, is that it?

He laughed. No, he said. There's hope for the Miwa. You've had your chance.

At a certain point the driver made another turn and took them through a series of quieter, darker streets, gunning the engine and checking his watch. A dog crossing the street looked up at the oncoming lights and swerved away at the last possible moment. In a perfect cone of light cast by a single bulb she saw a group of men seated on low stools around a table, play-ing chess, she thought, or cards; it was impossible to say what exactly. This is a long way to go for dinner, she said, but he was talking to the driver now, and either didn't hear her, or didn't bother to answer.

After another half-hour they pulled into a wide dirt field next to a kind of tent city: she saw a long, low series of roofs made out of plastic sheeting, glowing from lights underneath.

Parked all around them were lorries and pickup trucks, all covered in mud and dust, as if they'd just arrived from a long journey. She smelled frying food, garlic, oil, fish; her stomach cramped with hunger.

It's the weekend market, he said to her, as they climbed out of the van. People come here from all over Thailand to sell stuff. On Thursday nights, when just the vendors are here setting up—it's the biggest party in Bangkok. He took her elbow and led her down a narrow lane, between the tents; in the half-darkness, people hurrying past bumped into her and went on without speaking. Not a place you'd want to be on your own, he said. No one wants to see *farangs* around here without a good reason.

Do we have a good reason?

Absolutely. They stopped and he pushed aside a yellow plastic curtain, calling out a greeting in Thai. Two men and a woman stood up from a low folding table to greet them. The taller of the two was about her age, she guessed, had long hair in a ponytail, and wore jeans torn at the knees and a Chicago Bulls jersey. The other was much older, with a withered, creased face, and some sort of traditional garment, a shirt or jacket made of black homemade cloth with elaborate embroidery around the hems. And the woman couldn't have come up past her breastbone; her back was curved, and twisted slightly to one side, so she had a loping, asymmetrical limp. This is Charlie, Foster said, indicating the taller man, Sarpan, and Parang. At the mention of her name the woman gave Samantha a mischevious smile and fumbled with something hanging on a thin black cord around her neck. It was a small silver crucifix; she held it up so that everyone could see, and said something to Foster, who answered her quickly.

What did she say?

She asked if you were a Christian like us.

And how did you answer?

I said that you were a friend.

There was food already on the table, and a young woman came in through the back of the tent, bringing more dishes in stryrofoam bowls; somehow there were enough stools and overturned crates and boxes for everyone to sit on, and in a moment, without quite knowing how it happened, she was sitting squeezed in between Charlie and Parang, nibbling at a piece of roasted chicken smeared with hot pepper paste. Everyone seemed to be talking at once, and in the next tent some-one was playing loud pop music on a tinny radio; somehow it reminded her of being at the Kite and Whistle on a Friday night, packed shoulder to shoulder, shouting to be heard over the jukebox. Every so often Parang would touch her knee and smile, and gesture at something else she should eat: blackened shrimp on skewers, diced sour melon in some kind of sweet juice, sticky rice that had to be rolled into balls and eaten with grated green mango. She took the smallest pieces she could, and closed her eyes as the tastes exploded on her tongue, the saltiest, spiciest, sweetest, sourest, most bitter things she had ever eaten. This is how they make it when it's not for *farangs*, she thought. She felt giddiness coming over her, as if the ten-sion in her joints had been loosened a notch, like being drunk, but without the tinge of dizzy sickness after the third pint. You shouldn't be so relaxed, she thought. It isn't like you. But there it was again, the whole question of *like*. Like what? Like anything you've ever encountered?

That's why it made sense, not novelty, but openness. *Only connect*, as Forster said. It takes curiosity. It takes risk. Otherwise you'll be home in six months with a couple of shawls and some lousy snapshots.

Parang looped an arm around her back and rubbed her, inexplicably, between the shoulder blades. Her bottom teeth, Samantha saw, were all gold, one after another, incisors and bicuspids in a neat row.

So are these people Miwa? she shouted at Foster across the table. Is that how you know them?

He shook his head. These are Karen people, he said. They're how we get *to* the Miwa. Our transport. And our guides. Parang said something to him, and he nodded, vigorously; she reached under the table and brought up an orange shopping bag tied tightly at the top. She says she wants to show you some photos, he said. They took them on their last trip up there. Would you like to see them?

Of course.

The photographs, wrapped in newspaper and rubber bands, were brand new, still in their Kodak envelopes. She looked at each one with great care, conscious of the four sets of eyes staring at her. There was the kind of dense bright-green forest she had seen in Laos, thick bamboo groves and enormous ferns and banana palms; shaggy jungle mountainsides; a river the color of tea. A group of figures along a trail, carrying large loads on their backs, but the picture was taken at a great distance: it was impossible to tell one person from another. A village of houses on stilts; a naked girl of three or four look-ing fearfully at the camera, her fingers in her mouth. In the next picture, a group of barechested men, grinning, waving at the photographer. One held a cigarette between his lips. The picture was slightly out of focus, but she could see that all of them had long tattoos running up and down their arms, what appeared to be strings of words running vertically from wrist to shoulder.

Are these the Miwa? She showed him the picture, and he nodded. What are the tattoos for?

Oh, he said, some kind of spell. I'm not really sure. A good-luck totem.

She put one stack of photographs back into its envelope and opened another. The first was a picture taken just above the forest canopy—from the roof of a house, perhaps—of a plume of black smoke rising in the distance. The second showed a group of houses, or huts, on fire. It was bright day-light, and so the flames themselves were hardly visible: she could see the billowing white smoke, and the blackened tim-bers, and a strange blurring of the air around them, with the blue-orange tinge of the flame from a stove. Nobody could be seen. These houses, whosoever they were, were being left to burn to the ground.

In the third photo, a group of mud-smeared men squatted on a trail, with Kalashnikov rifles balanced over their knees or slung over their shoulders. This time the picture was focused, and she could see clearly the tattoos on their arms, the white threads bound around their wrists.

She looked up at Foster. He gave her a wistful smile and

shook his head.

You're not a missionary, she said. What is this, some kind of joke? These men are soldiers.

He took a packet of tissues from his shirt pocket and began to wipe his hands methodically. War is all part of the plan, he said. War *is* the plan. You've read the Bible, haven't you? Don't you know how it all ends?

But the Miwa don't know anything about that.

Don't patronize them, he said. You don't even know them. What, just because they haven't been given all your *advantages?* They know what the end of the world means. They've seen it happen. And, by Christmas, they want to be on the winning side.

She wanted to laugh; it was all a horrible joke, she thought, a put-on, some tribal war he had nothing to do with. Gallows humor, an aid worker's cynicism. But he stared at her with the same look of dry detachment and pity as ever.

You really don't know these things, do you?

What things?

Revelations nineteen, he said. *I saw heaven open, and a white horse appear; its rider was called Trustworthy and True, in uprightness he judges and makes war. From his mouth came a sharp sword with which to strike the unbelievers; he is the one who will rule them with an iron sceptre, and tread out the wine of Almighty God's fierce retribution.*

He translated the passage rapidly; Parang nodded, and Charlie put his hands together in the *wai* gesture and touched them to his forehead.

It's beautiful, isn't it? he said. *I saw an angel standing in the sun, and he shouted aloud to all the birds that were flying overhead in the sky,*

Come here, gather together at God's great feast. You will eat the flesh of kings, and the flesh of great generals and heroes—

Enough, she said. Enough!

She wanted to stand, but she was so tightly wedged in, with Parang's arm still looped around her waist, that there was no way to manage it without falling backwards, or turning over the table. Foster looked at her sorrowfully, his eyebrows tilted inward, his head tilted slightly to one side. I've seen that look before, she thought. The statue of Jesus outside the parish church in Mulder's Hill she passed every day on her way to school. *Suffer the children to come unto me.*

You're free to leave, of course, he said. In a minute. But there's a favor I'd like to ask of you first. Can you find your way back to the van?

The van?

There's a box in the back seat, he said, slowly, as if addressing a child. It's heavy, but you'll have to manage it by yourself, I'm afraid. Whatever you do, don't open it. And don't let it drop. Bring it here, and then Parang will give you an envelope, and you take that back to the van and put it in the glove compartment. The doors will be unlocked. Then the driver will take you back to pick up your things.

What is it? she asked. What's in the box?

Courage, he said. Pride. The Miwa aren't about to disappear without a fight. They're not willing to settle for a footnote in history. We've arranged a little event here in Bangkok that's going to take the struggle to the next level. We're going to cause an international incident.

I don't understand.

turns dangerous

The Lord has given us an extraordinary gift, he said, a once-in-a-lifetime opportunity. The last unguarded Israeli consulate, as it happens. Open to the public. At street level.

No, she said, loudly. She wanted to silence the table, to cut through the conversation volleying around her; she wanted them to see her alarm. Sarpan eyed her for a moment, picking at his teeth with a chicken bone, and turned away. You can't act this way, she said. You can't justify it, using these people as pawns. It's pathological.

Is it? He smiled, in a way that, she knew, he thought passed for irony. We're all pawns, my dear. In the end all wars become one war. That's God's plan.

Outside the tent, a group of drunken men passed by, singing in hoarse voices. Parang looked anxiously at her, her forehead creased, and reached up and put a hand to her cheek, speaking in a low voice. Samantha trembled.

What's she saying?

Afterward you'll know you played your part, too, he said. His face had softened, grown fine lines, like polished leather; it glowed, she thought, basking in some private, ineffable joy. She wants you to know that. Put yourself in God's hands. That's what she's saying. Do his bidding.

Inside the van, in the stifling heat, she lifted the box with great difficulty from its hiding place and set it on the rear seat. It was an ordinary cardboard carton, unmarked, closed at the top with heavy-duty copper staples; whatever was inside was about the weight of a stereo receiver or a small television. She pried two of the staples away with her fingernails, and ripped up a corner of one flap; a few styrofoam peanuts spilled out. Come on, she thought. I should know. Someone should know. The other staples came out easily, as if they hadn't been fixed properly, and then it was open, there on the seat, like an unexpected gift.

She pulled out a cylindrical metal device with a handle on one end, like a giant caulking gun, and then a kind of arm rest that looked as if it was meant to lock onto the cylinder. Underneath was something smooth and pointed at one end and very heavy. She put both hands around it, and lifted it, cradling it; it was a bomb, or some kind of short missile, painted a dull blue color, with a long number etched into one side. Her arms were shaking, but now that she had picked it up somehow she was terrified of putting it down. She sat back on her haunches and held it close to her chest, the sharp metal fins digging into the crook of her elbow.

What have I done with my life, she thought, that I should be here, in the back alley of a back alley of a sub-basement of Hell, holding certain death in my arms? Little droplets of sweat ran down her forehead and into the hollows of her eyes, and she blinked them away; she was used to sweating, if nothing else, after all this time. Is this the end coming, she thought, is this what it feels like? Is this Judgment? She remembered, out of nowhere, a bit of Exodus: *Moses said, Lord, surely you will not strike them all down?*

And the Lord said, *Stand aside.*

Merciful God, she thought, I'm sitting here all alone. Wouldn't this be the best way? She bent forward and wrapped herself around it, like a shell. Isn't this what you want? Not

praying

anonymous victims, but a single martyr, a martyr by her own free will? Against her skin, the metal was turning warm and slick; she hugged it closer to her chest, afraid of letting it slip. Do you feel it at all when it's this close, she wondered, do you feel heat, or do you just become transparent, and weightless. Do you feel it coming from outside your body, or are you the explosion, the bomb like another internal organ, nestled in your gut, somewhere north of the spleen and kidneys, beneath the lungs and the heart?

A full minute passed.

She was growing accustomed to its weight and solidity, to its tug of gravity. It seemed to her that she had spent her entire life learning the wrong things. She had no idea, for instance, how to lay the cables of a bridge so it could hold the weight of an army. She had not learned how to avoid being the instrument of men. But that's the wrong way to think about it, she told herself. There's no time like the present.

A missile has to fit into its launcher.

With trembling fingers she allowed it to rest on her knee, pointing straight up, and used her free hand to lift the cylinder into place beside it. It's a two-man job, she thought. This can't possibly be the manufacturer-recommended technique. She almost wanted to giggle. Holding the missile in the crook of her elbow, she let it slide down the tube, a little too hard. It latched into place with a loud click. She lifted the whole apparatus and set it against her shoulder, as if she'd been doing this her entire life, having never held a rifle, not even a toy one, having never *aimed* anything deadlier than a crumpled piece of paper at the bin. She swung so that it pointed in the direction she had come, the direction where Lloyd Foster would appear, when he noticed how long it had been, when he wondered what she was doing with his property. She would shut her eyes and cover her face, as soon as she saw him, against the breaking glass, and squeeze the trigger, and brace her body against the recoil. *Recoil.* A word she never thought would apply to her. She would wait till she saw his face again. She needed no other signal.

Dear Lord.

Amritsar

I don't like boats. For that matter, I don't like water, either, unless it's coming out of a tap, or a hose. Where would I have learned to swim, in the hot dusty Punjab of my childhood? We never traveled to the sea.

My children, grown up in a land laced with creeks and bays and rivers, find this an endless source of amusement. When they were little, they cajoled me into the deep end of the swimming pool, slithering and splashing as effortlessly as minnows. Always, on parents' day at summer camp, they insisted that I sit in the front seat of the canoe, white-faced, gripping the sides, while they paddled across the lake, just to show they could.

This is different, Ajay says.

My son, now 27, tall and barefoot in the bottom of a bass-fishing boat, holds out his hand for me to climb down from the dock.

This kind of boat is much more stable. There's no way we could capsize. And you can wear a life jacket if you want.

I sit on the dock's edge, hugging the piling the way a toddler holds his mother's skirt, and touch the boat's rail with one foot. It gives beneath my weight. From some long-ago class in materials engineering, I remember the physical properties of a liquid: an object is buoyed by a force equal to the weight of the liquid displaced by that object. For 23 years I've looked at our little bay as a pleasant backdrop, a guarantor of property values, a picturesque scene. But not *water* as such. And if I haven't seen this, what else haven't I seen?

Take my hand, Ajay says. Commands, rather. He's sweating; people are watching; he's impatient to get out into the breeze. Put your feet solidly on the deck, he says, and lean forward, and I'll hold you upright. Then you can sit down. You don't have to get up again.

It sounds easy enough. But my feet strike the floor harder than I intended; the hull slides from under me, slick as a bar of soap. I pitch forward, grasping the air, swallowing a howl of terror. Ajay jerks my sleeve, and miraculously the boat rights itself.

You see? It's not so difficult.

Don't mock me, I say. *You* would find it difficult if you were me.

And he looks at me with laughing eyes, this son, who has never known a barrier he couldn't leap, who will never have to do anything in his life he doesn't want to.

I was an obedient child. I was a sponge. From time to time, when I was young—after we left Chandigarh and moved to Delhi, where such things were uncommon enough to mention—I heard some adult whisper, She was there, in Amritsar—and I assumed it was an indication of great respect. I thought that Amritsar was a training school, a university for old shawl-wrapped aunties who could barely read.

The day was hot, as all April days are in north India. A Sunday, a Sikh festival day, in 1919. The two great Punjabi nationalists, Kitchlew and Satyapal, had just been arrested, and three days before, a riot had occurred in the center of the city. Banks had been burned, a few unfortunate Englishmen killed by mobs. Nonetheless, that day some 20,000 people packed into the Jallianwallah Bagh, a large public market and square in the middle of the city, surrounded by high walls, with only one entrance.

They were not protesters. They were shopping and eating and saying prayers and listening to busking musicians and traveling salesmen and Congress party organizers. It was, after all, a holiday. Indians, then and now, do not take Sundays off. We have no concept of a weekly day of rest. So one takes advantage of a break in schedule—even three days after a riot, even in the midst of a gathering war.

An English general, Dyer, marched fifty soldiers into the entranceway of the Bagh, making escape impossible. Without announcing himself, without ordering the crowd to disperse, he instructed his soldiers to fire. The massacre lasted ten minutes. Three hundred and seventy-nine unarmed men, women, and children died, some shot, some trampled underfoot as the crowd panicked and ran from one side of the square to the other. More than a thousand were injured. Afterward, Dyer ordered his soldiers to retreat, without summoning ambulances.

In my family—my parents both working frantically to climb the ranks of the civil service into middle-class respectability—this was no more than a fact, a date in time, as dry and removed as any other words on the shabby paper of our history books. But when I was 10 and 11 years old, my best friend was a boy named Gopal Singh. We became friends at school because neither one of us liked to play cricket. Instead, we sat on a dusty patch of grass in one corner of the school yard, in the shade of a mango tree that grew on the other side of the wall, and tried to best each other with elaborate lies. I was much taken with *The Ramayana*, and my specialty was wild speculations about what would happen to Sampati and Hanuman and all the rest in present-day India; I delighted in turning Kaikeyi and the evil maid, Manthara, into Bollywood actresses, and Ravana into a Bombay gangster. Gopal was more of a literalist; his stories were always plausible and thus all the more vivid and grotesque. In particular, he maintained that he was a descendant of Udham Singh, the Punjabi folk hero who took revenge for Amritsar, for those 379 innocent souls. He gunned down Michael O'Dwyer—the governor of Punjab during the massacre—at Caxton Hall, in London, in 1940.

That's just the beginning of the story, Gopal would say, the *rest* has been *ruthlessly* suppressed. He loved to trill his *R*'s in imitation of certain politicians whose long speeches in English were often broadcast on the radio. Udham Singh was *not* captured, as is claimed. In Gopal's version, he escaped over the prison wall with a rope ladder concealed underneath his jacket, hid himself among the crates of china on a freight train bound for London, and lived underground for years in the city, like Jack the Ripper, carrying out a campaign of murder and mutilation on the O'Dwyer family and the families of his superiors. The devastation was total, Gopal liked to say. None of the murderers' families escaped untouched.

Not until we were years older and our conversations had moved on to other topics—exams, colleges, imagined girl-friends—did I notice how Gopal's talk kept veering, ineluctably, back to Amritsar. In his corner of the room he shared with his two younger brothers, he kept a photograph of Udhamji in a carved sandalwood frame, and in front of it the spent casings of two rifle bullets his uncle in the Army had sent him from the Chinese border in the Himalayas. Gopal, I finally said one day, when we were perhaps fifteen, it isn't right, worshipping him like a god. He was just one person. And anyway, he shot O'Dwyer in the back.

By then, Gopal's face had lost its preadolescent puffiness and had in fact become quite tight and angular, even wizened, as if he was underfed, or smoked too many bidis, though I knew he didn't smoke at all. He looked at me and flashed a ravenous grin. You don't understand, he said. Udhamji was the only one who stood up to the *angreezis*. He was the one true Sikh. The one true Indian.

But if you read about Gandhiji and Nehru—

I'm not talking about *history*, he said, waving his hand dismissively. I'm talking about *blood*. *Innocent blood*. It could have been us. Our mothers, our sisters. Doesn't that matter?

It was almost 50 years ago, I told him.

Everything is boring today, he said, scratching his nose, as if it was an unpleasant growth he wished he could remove. Everything is just *work*. I can't help it. I was born at the wrong time, I think. India doesn't need me.

The phrase came back to me, like a stinging slap, the day

I picked up my visa papers from the American Embassy. Of course, I should have said scornfully, India doesn't need any of us. India eats us like tinned sardines and spits out the bones. But by then Gopal had gone off to a trade school in Agra, and I thought I would never see him again.

Why, until this unhoped-for day, have I never learned to slide an iridescent jelly worm, a strange, slippery bit of silicone, onto a tiny jabbing hook that would prefer to bury itself in my fingertip, or to tie delicate knots with 10-pound filament, as if I was stitching lace, or to choose the proper size for the proper red-and-white plastic bobber? Being a radiologist, I've never had a way with scalpels and hoses and stitches and flesh. Everyone else on the staff at St. Joseph's fished and plays golf, save myself and Talal Mohammed and Eliot Rubenstein. We go to the symphony, and eat our wives' elaborate dinners, and celebrate one another's holidays: Diwali, Eid, Chanukah. We do not need to prove our masculinity by killing things wantonly, sloppily, and lazily—or, in this case, not killing them, but torturing them for sport in the sun.

Why indeed, if not that Ajay is marrying Christine Farrell, who grew up three doors down from us, whose parents, Tom and Melinda, we've known some 20 years. *Known* is perhaps stating it too strongly. We see them raking leaves in their yard, across the aisle at PTA meetings, on opposite sides of a barbecue at a block party. She teaches the second grade over in Aberdeen, near the military base, and he runs a small construction company, mostly specialty work, installing $50,000 kitchens with marble countertops and those absurd steel refrigerators you see in magazines, in the new housing developments in Fallston and Bel Air.

In a way, this familiarity makes things no easier. One wants neighbors to remain neighbors, not to move into the house and scatter their newspapers and laundry about, not to become family, as if our street is its own little village. Tom is a Vietnam veteran who returned to college but dropped out, a reader of military history, a subscriber to dozens of magazines, and is well-informed but desperately, painfully, shy. When we are together, alone, our conversation quickly dwindles into silence. We grow shifty-eyed, vaguely guilty, and seek out Teja and Melinda, who always have something to say to one another.

So I have decided that our point of contact, our common ground, will be fishing. But first I have to learn on my own. It wouldn't do for one father-in-law to be the abject pupil of the other.

Find a shallow place, I say to Ajay, as he guides us away from the dock upstream, and he rolls his eyes and wipes sweat from his lip with the back of his arm.

It's *all* shallow, he says, don't you know, Dad, the whole river's not more than six feet deep. You could walk across it if you had to.

On days like this, I have more and more difficulty seeing him as one who came from my loins and Teja's small belly. Five-foot-eleven, taller than anyone in my family, taller than any Indian I know, he's kept his lacrosse-player physique, the broad shoulders and narrow waist and calves like bunched fists. The wearing of the turban was never really an issue. We cut his hair when he went into kindergarten. Until the age of 12, he answered us in Punjabi at home, in private; then he switched to English, and we pretended not to notice. Some children are like that: their Americanness is built into their physiognomy, into their very being. And why not? They are here, after all, not there. For them it isn't a question of adaptation.

Now he's obscurely angry with me. Not because I'm an obstinate old fool, who keeps turning in his seat to wave at him to *slow down*. And not because I made an intemperate remark the other day about the cost of the honeymoon he's planning. Ten days in St. Kitts, I said. For that much you could go on a month's first-class tour of Rajasthan.

He's angry at me, yes. But I wonder if even he knows why.

The story, as I understand it, goes like this: Christine and Ajay and Preeta were all very close as children, sharing toys in the sandbox and racing their Big Wheels up and down Landing Lane. (That much *I* remember, though Teja claims that during my residency and fellowship I missed the first six years of my children's lives entirely. I remember paying for the pizza at their pizza parties and I remember tending to Christine when she skinned her knee on the back patio—she must have been seven or eight—with Betadine and Q-tips, stroking her shoulder, kissing her forehead as she wailed.) Then, some years later, she vanished from our lives. I asked after her once, and Preeta rolled her eyes and said, She's such a stoner, a complete space case. She had a boyfriend who drove around the neighborhood in a purple van with the windows painted over and no muffler. I remember catching sight of her, once or twice, dashing in or out of her parents' house, dressed all in black and wearing cartoonishly huge pants, her hair dyed red or pink or black.

We've never discussed it with Tom and Melinda, of course. I have no idea how she came to realize that there was no future in pretending to be a ghost, or a corpse, or a heroin addict, or whatever it was those girls wanted to be. She survived, with no visible damage. Perhaps we should all just be happy with that.

Christine is a tall, lovely girl, very typically American in some ways; she has thin hands, wide-set eyes, and wavy hair the color of teak, and is always changing it, growing it long or chopping it short, adding colors, having it straightened, or cut so that it looks like an accident. This is a topic of constant conversation between Teja and Preeta. She stays most of the time at Ajay's apartment in Hunt Valley, but is always *dropping by*, as she says, now that the wedding approaches, particularly around four or five in the afternoon, when Teja bustles around the kitchen, making roti or chopping things for dinner. She sits at one of the bar stools and drinks Teja's terrible instant coffee, and they talk—about what, I'm never sure. I have no interest in disturbing their fragile communion. If I happen to be home, I take the newspaper and go into the living room to watch the early news.

Teja, I say sometimes, she wants you to teach her. You need to offer, not just let her sit and watch. Start with something simple. Start with dal.

Teja shakes her head vigorously. If she wants to learn, she needs to ask, she says. She has to be assertive. It won't just fall into her lap. She has to make the effort.

But she's shy. And you move too fast.

Tough, she says. If an Indian woman doesn't move fast, she'll spend twenty four hours a day in the kitchen.

It's true that Indian cooking *is* very difficult to learn. Teja keeps her spices in a jumble of bags and boxes and peanut-butter jars, none labeled. I myself have no idea what goes into what. When she goes away for a few days at her sister's in West Orange, she leaves the freezer packed with two or three weeks' worth of food.

My fear, I suppose, is that Christine is trying to learn by osmosis. I sometimes wonder whether she wants to be Indian, in the way that so many Americans want to be something they aren't. Not long ago she mentioned, very casually, that wedding dresses are so expensive, so difficult to fit and choose,;wouldn't it just be easier if she wore a red sari, one size fits all? Teja was making *poori* and nearly burned the tips of her fingers off in hot oil. When she recovered from the shock, she said, I still have mine. You can try it on sometime if you like. As far as I know, the conversation ended there.

There's more to it than that, of course.

Whenever I see Christine—this young, coltish girl, this slender, mild-featured beauty, my daughter-in-law in a few months' time, mother (with a little luck) of my grandchildren—I think, S*and nigger*. With a certain crinkling in the back of my neck.

Sand nigger.

The phrase appeared one day on Preeta's locker when she was in the seventh grade, painted, naturally, in Wite-Out. She scratched it off with her house key. The principal—a very nice man, Ripley was his name, but hapless, his hair combed in an elaborate vortex to disguise his baldness—accused her of defacing her locker and assigned her detention. Ajay got wind of it at lunchtime. He stormed into Ripley's office, full of seventeen-year-old righteousness, accused him of covering up a hate crime, of blaming the victim, of fostering a climate of racism. An overly aggressive vice-principal intervened; there was shoving; there was a half-thrown punch. The police were called.

When I promised no lawsuits, no letters to the national press or calls to the ACLU, Ajay received three days' suspension and a fine for disruptive behavior on school property.

Half a lifetime of good feelings—of birthday parties, of school musicals, of graduation awards—isn't undone by a child's puerile phrase. Not even a real insult, but a kind of comic mutation. Hate lacks imagination. Hate never made art, only dreary clichés. And still! I can't manage to rid my mind of *sand nigger*. In Christine's creamy, honey-colored skin, in the slight depression of her scapula, itself like a tiny desert landscape, is something that evokes the phrase.

I won't deny that I've looked for that something. Or that my eyes, when she turns with a practiced swing of the head so that her hair describes a flat arc in the air, linger an instant too long as she saunters toward the door. Or that Teja becomes snappy when I enter the room, and flicks bits of coriander at me off the tips of her fingers, and assigns me to take out the newspapers for recycling. We all have bad habits.

Everything's fine, they kept saying to us when we called. Preeta in her dormitory room at Tufts, barely moved in, two weeks into the school year; Ajay down in his lab at Hopkins, finishing a project on cyclic radiotherapies. They were distant, shocked, a little oblivious, not willing to allow the event to knock their lives off course even for a moment. Yes, I saw it on TV, they said. Yes, it's terrible.

Teja and I had been sitting on the couch all afternoon, unable to move from that terrible blue glare, not even getting up to make tea or turn on a light. When one station went to a commercial, Teja automatically clicked to the next. The phone rang, and I wiped my mouth and blinked, several times, as if I had been asleep, before pulling myself upright and crossing the room.

Pull down your shades, said my best friend, Sanjay Bhose, speaking from his cell phone in Indiana, without even saying hello. Close all the curtains. Turn the lights off. Put a mattress in the basement and sleep down there tonight.

Sanu, I said, don't be ridiculous. Our neighbors know who we are.

Really? What do they know exactly, you fool? That you wear a turban and carry a knife everywhere? You think anyone's making hard-and-fast distinctions these days?

We've been here for 20 years, for God's sake, I said. We were the only Indian family in the whole town for a decade.

Look on any of the Web sites, he said. Attacks on Sikhs are happening everywhere. Look—for Teja's sake, don't be a fool! I don't have long. I have 25 more people to call. When it comes down to it, you know we're all dirty Arabs to them. Don't take a chance.

When I hung up the phone I murmured to Teja, That was Sanjay, just checking in, and said nothing more, but immediately climbed the stairs to the third floor and went into Ajay's room, still decorated with his wrestling and swimming trophies, his System of a Down and Rage Against the Machine posters, and opened the window that allows access onto the roof over the kitchen, and climbed out, scratching my arm badly on the windowsill. It must have been around 7:30. The sunset had a pale, milky quality, like sherbet. Earlier, the day had been blazing hot, and it was just beginning to cool; the air was full of the smell of drying grass and leaves, hot asphalt—our street had just been repaved—and the slight, sour smell of the bay at low tide. Our house is at the end of a cul-de-sac, on a slight rise, with woods behind us, and from that vantage point I could see many of the roofs of Lord Calvert Way and Landing Lane, clear down to the public swimming pool at the corner of Schoolhouse Street, and the long grass lane that leads off to the high school on the other side of that road. Nobody was stirring, it seemed. At a time like this you would think that people would come out of their houses and scream, or tear their clothes, or just weep and stare at televisions together, but we live in a suburb, of course, a place without a center—no City Hall, no Boston Common, no village church. Nobody would know where to go. All this pain and anguish, and no place to put it.

Not for another hour, after our stomachs had finally started to rumble, did Teja stand up from the couch and notice Tom Farrell's truck backed into our driveway.

We could see through the back window of his cab that he was on the driver's side, and his son, Colin, was sitting shotgun. It had never occurred to me what the phrase meant, until that moment, when I saw that they both had rifles across their laps, the barrels sticking out of the windows on each side, and that a third gun was on the rack behind their heads.

Most of my neighbors are hunters. On one or two occasions we've had to eat the gristly and dry wild ducks or geese they've killed—gingerly, because the shot can crack a tooth. But until that night I had never seen a gun displayed in our neighborhood, out in the open air. I had never realized I hated firearms with such a passion. My eyeballs felt as if they were being boiled in a pan. The craziness, I thought, the recklessness of bringing them into public view, on a day like today. As if we needed to be reminded of the lethal possibilities of a few carefully joined bits of steel.

Teja stood very still in a corner of the living room, her face fixed in a rictus of surprise. This isn't their job, she said. They will just call attention. Go tell them to go away.

It would be tempting to say that I was returned to another life, an earlier life, where, for example, I once saw a harijan, an untouchable, a little boy, beaten nearly to death in a village where my bus had stopped for a tea break. But in truth I felt no connection with any previous point in my life at all. I was dissolved, a packet of sugar in a glass of water. People say that America is closer to heaven than anywhere on Earth, and in a way this is true: heaven becomes your nearest point of comparison. Which is to say, no comparison is possible.

Teja, I said, that man is our friend.

Your friend. *Your* friend! To me, no different from all the other lunatics.

Then at least be glad we have one lunatic with a gun on *our* side.

Coward, she hissed, stepping toward me, with her pal raised. Coward! Go out there and tell them!

I caught her wrist and slapped her, quickly, lightly. I had never done such a thing before, nor even imagined it. My fingers raised a red imprint on her cheek.

So this is the kind of man you are, she said, clenching her fists. I should never have married you.

That night she slept in the front seat of our Ford station wagon in the garage, wrapped in a parka and a blanket, ready to flee a moment after waking, clasping the door handle as if it, too, was a weapon.

I met Gopal Singh for the last time in the cocktail bar of the Ambassador Hotel in New Delhi. I was home on vacation from school, escorting Babuji to a retirement party for one of his colleagues; this job fell to me in the years after my mother's death, when my brother and sister were already married, with jobs and children. Once my father was seated at the table of honor, gin-and-tonic in hand, I excused myself and retreated to the fringes of the crowd, hoping to find someone my own age—a girl, of course, preferably—to talk to. Instead I brushed past Gopal, grim-faced, in a tight waiter's tuxedo, carrying a silver tray loaded with pakoras and chutney. He had a spray of acne scars across both cheekbones and his skin seemed two shades more sallow, but still, he was he and I was I, and we took three steps apart and simultaneously turned to face each other, like gunfighters in an old Western. Gurukha, he said, holy moly. What are you doing here?

I met him later that night at a tea stand outside, on Panjali

Road, having asked some old friends to give my father a ride home. Gopal had changed into a dirty white kurta and dungarees; he kept the tuxedo on his lap, under his elbows, folded up in a wrinkled plastic tailor's bag, as if he was afraid someone might snatch it away. I insisted on buying him dinner, and he dipped his poori into the chole and gobbled away rudely, as if he hadn't eaten in days. While he ate I explained that I had a fellowship and a special visa to study X-ray technology in the U.S.A., in Fairfax, Virginia.

Fairfax, he said, nodding in recognition. A Fairfax was in command of the 39th Fusiliers. They occupied Srinagar and murdered a whole houseful of congressmen in the summer of '21.

You always had a mind for those dates and facts, I said. I could never keep it straight. The whole history of Independence—I suppose it never seemed that relevant to me. But you knew better.

Independence, he said, in English, pronouncing each syllable distinctly, his eyes flickering with each bicycle and Ambassador taxi passing by. Isn't it funny? We think we achieved it back in '47. As if it was simply a muddle about which flag goes at the top of the pole.

What else is it, then?

I've been taking this class over in Saroj Nagar, he said. Given for free by the New Communist Party. We started out reading Marx, the classic stuff. Lenin. *To the Finland Station*. And now this. He reached into his back pocket and handed me a greasy paperback. *Black Skin, White Masks* was the title, The author in small black letters, a funny, French-sounding name.

It's all about the psychology of the blacks, he said. The post-colonials. It's about psychic liberation and the thought-habits of the oppressed.

Gopal, I said, *bhaiya*, don't tell me you're becoming a politician. I expected more of you. I smiled, but it was a feeble attempt at a joke.

Do you think if I wanted to be one of those apparatchiks I'd be working here? he asked. There's no struggle anymore in Delhi. It's all sahibs trading favors. Indiraji has us by the throat. I'm saving money these days. In six months I'm headed to Bihar.

Don't joke with me, I said. What, you want to be a Naxalite? A guerilla with your face painted in the bush? Listen, get hold of your senses, Gopal. You're a middle-class Punjabi, just like me. We're no different. They'll eat you alive.

Gurukha, he said, there's only one truth. The world is going to be made over from the bottom up. Trust in what I'm saying. There is only one possible future. The 20th century tells us that.

Maybe, I said. It was a futile argument, I could see that much. I was tired, and a little disappointed that Gopal hadn't been more impressed with me. I was done with India, and impatient to move on.

You don't agree with me, he said. Of course you don't. His eyes took on a kind of oily sheen, and he grinned. That's all right. I knew you would never have done it. I always knew it, even back in those days.

Done what, *bhaiya*?

Take revenge, of course. Like Udhamji. Even if I handed

you the pistol. You could never shoot a man in the back. Even for the honor of your whole nation. And that's what we need, don't you see? We have to shoot them in the back. There will never be a balance of power. We have the morality of slaves.

Gopal, I said, my good friend, Nothing will be solved that way. It's a new world. There are too many possibilities to ignore.

Thin as he was—emaciated, really—his face had lost none of its old expressiveness. He fixed me with a look that was at once stricken and proud, his eyes shining like fresh wounds. It was as though I could see him disappearing into memory before my eyes; as though, if I got up to embrace him, he would no longer be there.

You keep that feeling, he said. America is a land of dreamers, no? May you get what you truly deserve.

With that he wiped his mouth on his sleeve and went to look for his bicycle.

There's an art to it, Ajay says.

He crooks back the wire that holds the line in place with his index finger, and flicks the rod so that the hook, with its weights and bobs attached—the tackle, it's called, a word I never knew before today—arcs across the water and drops 50 feet away with hardly a splash. He hands the rod to me. Now hold it gently, he says, and pay attention with your hands. Any slight vibration could be a hit. Just the smallest tug. Use the reel sparingly, don't get all excited. It's not *Jaws*, you know. You have to play the fish. You have to make it think it isn't caught.

Like marketing, I say.

I should learn to be more philosophical. Clinical practice is a fool's gamble these days. And Ajay wants to start a family; he wants Christine to drive a Land Rover and not work. So instead of being a proper doctor and seeing patients, he flies around the country conducting seminars for Pfizer, and pretends that no one knows the difference, especially me. He thinks that calling it *practitioner education* makes it just another teaching job. And when I make my sniping comments, he never responds, never reacts, just looks in the other direction and waits for the moment to pass. As if I've farted.

It's good that you have hobbies, I say. I never did.

He laughs. No one uses that word anymore. When I think of *hobby* I think of someone in his basement using a wood-burning set or painting watercolors.

Then what would you call it?

I don't know. Something more serious. A passion.

This? My voice sounds unpleasant and shrill, like a woman on television. I don't believe it. Your children are your passion. Your wife. Your career. Maybe your political views could be a passion. Not *fishing*.

Well, I think that's a narrow way of looking at the world.

I hope not. I hope it's a matter of changing vocabulary.

What do you mean?

Nothing, I say, wishing he were a little quicker on the uptake. Look. You're feeling sensitive. Your mother and I both know it. You imagine us saying terrible, censorious things behind your back. You think we're angry because you never even discussed an arrangement with us.

I know you better than that.

Cut the crap, I say, which startles him so much he nearly drops his rod. Let's be honest. How could you not be a little scared? It's easy for you now. But it won't always be easy. Your children—what will they be, exactly? Are we to call them half-Sikhs?

Why not? Would you mind?

It isn't just what I think but what the world thinks that matters. Some things can't be so easily combined.

People of my generation don't look at it that way, he says. That's what you're missing. That's the least important thing about her, in my eyes. Look, it's a different world now. Everyone's mixing it up. In 20 years nobody will be anything anymore.

I don't know which makes me angrier: the poverty of the sentiment, or the vacuous way Ajay has with words, the way he slops them around like a child carrying water in a pail. It's enough to make one wish for an older, stricter, cheaper kind of education, rather than the one we paid so many tens of thousands of dollars for.

It must be pleasant for you, I say. I feel my tongue loosening in my throat, coming free of its moorings. Now that you've forgotten what it's like to be called a sand nigger.

His eyelids draw back like a frog's, or a fish's, some unblinking reptilian thing. Dad, he says, what the fuck has gotten into you?

Don't talk to me that way.

He's reeling in his line with quick, jabbing motions, his lower lip jutting out uncontrollably, like a child's. The trip is ruined, the day is ruined, and now my throat is full of bile, thinking of what he'll say to Teja, what he'll tell Christine, my God.

No, no, no, I say. Look, I was being provocative. I don't want you to be naive.

He throws the rod down at his feet, heedless of the barb quivering at its end.

I was the one who got handcuffed and stuffed in the police car, he says, with the guys on the radio talking about the towelhead who went psycho at the middle school. *I* was the one who heard the jokes about Indiana Jones and how I wanted to tie girls up and tear their hearts out. *You* chose to move to this fucking hick town. And now you're stuck, and you're jealous.

Of course, I say. They would never arrest a Sikh in Hunt Valley.

I don't have time for this, he says, his eyes skittering impatiently over the river behind me. I played lacrosse at Hopkins, for God's sake. My friends are lawyers, prosecutors, ADAs. Nobody could ever touch me. Anyway, I'm not the one with the stack of *Playboys* filed away behind the old bills in the garage. Not a lot of Indian *larkis* in *Playboy*, are there? I wonder why, then.

My eyes are beginning to water.

Oh, come on, he says. Not now, Dad. Don't turn it around on me.

We weren't disagreeing.

Whatever it was, then. And by the disgusted look on his face, I can see that he still has no idea what we've been fighting about. How hard it is for the lucky, the young, the successful, to consider the alternative, to imagine what might bring them and their theories and their elaborate defenses, like Icarus, to

Earth!

Just be safe. And make Christine safe. That's your first priority. Don't forget it.

Whatever you say, Dad.

Not for the first time in my life, I feel like an actor in a commercial. Promise me, I say, knowing he won't, knowing I wouldn't accept it if he did.

Having found it only late in my lifetime, you could say I believe strongly in harmony. An outdated concept, you might say. It carries with it a strong whiff of the Beatles and that terrible Coca-Cola commercial I watched with the children when they were young. But, of course, a marriage relies on harmony, a family is composed of nothing but it, and perhaps, if I may speechify for a moment, this is why I never bought the children separate TVs, though we could afford them, and most of their friends had them—separate TVs in every room, facing the bed. I wanted them to fight over what to watch.

I am learning to fish because the components of a harmony change over time. Because the song changes, if you'll excuse the terrible analogy. Not because of what happened three years ago last November, when we were over at the Farrells' for dinner, when Teja and Melinda were frying chicken in the kitchen, and Tom stood up from the couch, apropos of nothing, and said, Come into the garage, I've got something I want to show you. I followed him down the steps into the damp, gas-smelling darkness, him pulling the cord on one dim bulb after another, until he stopped at his workbench. There, lying atop a green chamois cloth, was a pistol, an enormous black automatic pistol, shiny with fresh oil.

It isn't loaded, he said. Pick it up.

It was heavier than I thought it would be, of course, having only seen criminals waving the plastic ones on TV. I have long fingers, and it fit into my hand surprisingly well. Hardly knowing what I was doing, I gripped the handle with all four fingers and lifted it a few inches, not wanting to touch the trigger.

This is how you see if it's loaded, he said. This is where the clip goes in. Always point it away from yourself and away from the floor.

I touched the trigger gently with my fingertip and straightened my arm.

If you want, I can take you to a shooting range next Sunday. Say we're going to Home Depot. Teja doesn't have to know. Though she ought to, sure. She just doesn't *have* to.

Tom, I said, I can't have a firearm in my house. I'm a doctor.

He looked as if I had told him that no, I can't drive a car, because my feet are size 11 and my name starts with *G*.

Listen, he said, we all know what happened back in September.

We're very grateful.

I don't want you to be grateful. I want you to be prepared. There'll be a next time, and a next time. Maybe when you're out seeing a movie. Maybe when you stop to get gas. You people ought to know what you're up against.

You may be right. And then having a pistol seems even more useless, doesn't it?

He stared at me so intently that I thought I could see his eyeballs protruding, like the women with goiters you see in any alleyway in India.

Man, he said, you're missing something. This isn't a joke.

And then, without knowing why, I began to laugh.

It was horribly embarrassing. I clutched at my sweatered stomach, not knowing how to stop. Tom looked genuinely alarmed. After all, a weapon was there, between us—unloaded, but it makes no difference, really. A weapon is a symbol. Its power is not diminished by its practical uselessness.

In fact, of course, a weapon is always useless.

That was part of why I was laughing. We men inhabit this world with such solemnity! Such ominous forecasts! Such elaborate mechanisms of defense and safety! And then go on smoking and eating cheeseburgers and driving 80 miles per hour and waving firearms around like toys.

I think you should leave, Tom said. In a hurry now, folding the cloth over the gun like a shroud. Turning his back to me, but not so quickly that I couldn't see his mouth knitted in boyish disappointment. *I thought you might be one of us*, he was thinking; I knew it as plainly as if he'd said the words aloud. *Aren't you one of us?*

And who am I, after all, I was thinking, to put on airs, to refuse to join this fellowship of wishful criminals?

Tom, I sputtered, I can't leave. We have to go upstairs and eat your fried chicken.

That earned me a sidelong glance, a pursed, sour-lemon smile.

You'll think about it, then.

I promise I'll think about it.

And we went up the stairs, turning out one light after another, into the bright rooms and the sound of our wives' voices, the smell of frying things, which to all human beings is the smell of happiness. We have never discussed it since.

Nobody Ever Gets Lost

PATERSON, N.J.: A coroner's inquest has found that corrosion was the cause of death in an accident involving two sisters, ages 7 and 11, who were crushed to death when the roof of the elevator in their apartment building collapsed Tuesday. Linda and Micaela Hernandez were the daughters of the building superintendent, Martín Hernandez, who had been hired a month before. Paterson police said that no criminal charges have been filed in connection with this incident.

She raises her eyes from the paper. Broadway is strangely quiet: a few taxis swishing by, a jet's rumble, a baby wailing somewhere down the block. The Indian man at the newsstand jingles a handful of coins absentmindedly. For a moment the world seems to hesitate—an expectant pause—and then speeds up again with a soft *pop*. She clasps the newspaper under her arm and grips the handrail on the subway stairs, light and dizzy as a ball of twine unraveling.

On the train, tucked safely against the wall in the front of the car, she turns back to the front page and starts again: New incursions in Ramallah; the stock market down two-and-a-half percent. Weapons inspectors kicked out of Iraq; tuberculosis on the rise in U.S. prisons. Her eyes skitter across the paragraphs. *No criminal charges.* As if that's all there is to it, as if that's the end of the story. *Corrosion was the cause of death.* Is that a sentence, she wonders, is that allowed to stand as an actual statement of fact? *Corrosion* is the cause of death?

And how does an elevator roof collapse?

It must have been on the ground floor, or in the basement. Otherwise the cable would have kept the roof in place and the car would have fallen to the bottom of the shaft. Did the cable break? Did the pulley fall?

She looks up and down the car. It's 9:45: the busy people, the commuters, the newspaper-readers, have disappeared. Across from her a glassy-eyed teenaged boy nods to the beat from his headphones, picking at his braids; two seats down a young woman in hospital scrubs sleeps with her head tilted back against the window.

Life goes on, in its unquestioning, unsurprised way. Isn't that what we're supposed to be doing? Trundling back and forth, like ants in the busy anthill: sick of grief, sick of outrage. Barely glancing at a headline here and there. Going on, and letting the experts handle the rest. The ruins aren't even there anymore; she saw a picture the other night, on the late news. An empty box, polished and clean, anonymous as a planter. *It has gone on. It is going on. It will go on.* How many ways can you say it? *Il continue. Accende. Se enciende. A avansa. Vai sobre.*

Innocent little verbs, she thinks, it isn't your fault you turn my stomach.

These little tragedies are inevitable.

Roger's voice has been coming out of nowhere: little bright flashes, half-second migraines, gone before she can grope in her bag for the Tylenol. She closes her eyes and rubs her temples. *The statistics require it. If you take eight million people and pack them together in a few square miles of concrete and glass, what else could possibly happen?* He liked to say that when he was fixing one of her window slides, standing on a chair and leaning out over the sill, eleven stories up. By rights, he would say, if you break this thing enough times, eventually I'll slip and fall out. You should have me insured.

And she would say, Then I'd have to decide whether to sit here or push you and take the cash.

Oh, that's no contest at all. He was never more than half-capable of joking about money. You know what my projected worth would be? Seriously. You could actually buy this apartment, for one thing. You might actually make it to retirement.

He always sounded so calm, so unflappable, that was the irresistible part; and then there was the high horse, the way his voice went reedy and nasal at the upper ranges, the Midwestern tendency to lecture. *Just don't sit there paralyzed*, he'd say, when she came home ranting about having to translate another Beaujolais Nouveau press release. *Turn the page. Every day is a test of your strength.* She hated his little Nietzschean proverbs, but he could never resist sneaking them in when she offered the least resistance. Your life is a motivational poster, she told him once. You actually *believe* that shit. And what did he say in return? There's nothing wrong with having a philosophy to live by.

Try just living, she said. I'll take just living, if you don't mind. One day. One day. One day. Another day.

You're so afraid of sentimentality you'd rather not plan for anything at all.

Try having an original thought, then. One that doesn't taste like it came straight out of the can.

That was in 1999, the summer of their engagement, which she'd insisted they treat like a pregnancy and not reveal until the fourth month, thank god: so it could be allowed to die and slip away without a whisper, unlike a lot of other bad ideas of late.

Always, when they were lazing around her apartment on those Sundays, he wore the same pair of jeans, which he kept there for that purpose. The crotch was ripped open, the cuffs disintegrating. During the week she kept them folded at the bottom of her underwear drawer. She wanted to walk around impregnated with his scent. Even during their breaks, their lacunae, he called them, the jeans stayed in place, like a sachet.

And so: it's September again. She hasn't opened that drawer in a year. Her new underwear stays folded in neat stacks in a shopping bag in the closet.

Now that he's gone, she thinks, does that mean he was wrong? Does that mean he lost the argument?

At work she folds the newspaper with the article facing up and lays it to one side at her desk, on a stack of journals she's been meaning to read for months. It isn't a particularly busy day. She's just finished the business plan of an Italian pharmaceutical company, and her inbox is briefly, blessedly empty. To look busy she shops online for the latest edition of the *Trans-*

lator's Dictionary of Weights and Measures and tries to open the *Romania Libera* website, which has been shut down for days.

Who were crushed to death.

Lately she's been thinking about going back to graduate school, picking up where her master's thesis left off: a translation of the correspondence between two sixteenth-century Jesuits, one in Barcelona, one in Bucharest, who believed that Catalan and Romanian were evolving, rather regressing, back to the spoken Latin of the late empire. A topic so obscure no one would fund her to pursue it further. But now, she thinks, I've got savings, I could carry myself on that for awhile.

What she wants most desperately is to have her carrel back: that cubicle on the twelfth floor of the library, with its tiny key and flimsy lock, and all around it, on every side, the infinite network of possible knowledge, directions, propositions. *El jardin de senderos que se bifurcan,* Borges called it. For that she'd gladly give up her pension plan, her weekly manicure, even her office, with its window that faces the dusky brick wall of the building next door, a color that changes as the light changes. In the late afternoons, when the rays of the setting sun fall into that gap, the bricks glow, a deep, rich, purplish shade. She wishes she could ban it from the color spectrum, from the gradations of visible light, and hold it captive there, like a goldfish in a closet that you open only once a day.

In the kitchen, getting her third cup of coffee, she sees Donald Wu rummaging in the refrigerator, sniffing old boxes of carryout and throwing them away. Donald is an engineer, a quiet, fastidious man who translates Chinese technical manuals, who

always smiles faintly at her in the hallways. Last September—
she has no idea how he knew—a card from him appeared in
her mailbox, a folded sheet of craft paper with Chinese char-
acters written in lashing calligraphy across the front. Inside, it
said, *The whole world is crying.* His name was not signed, and she
has never known how to thank him.

Donald, she says, I have a question you might be able to
answer.

Yes? His voice is muffled by the refrigerator.

I'm trying to find out how elevators work.

He stands up, opening a Domino's box, making a face at it.
An elevator, he says. That's about the simplest kind of machine
there is. Just a pulley with a box attached. Ninety percent of
elevator problems are with the ordering system, the electron-
ics. A mechanical elevator will hardly ever break down, unless
it isn't lubricated properly. He scratches the wispy hairs that lie
across his scalp. Is yours on the fritz or something?

There was this article in the paper, she says. An elevator accident in New Jersey. Two little girls were killed. The roof of
the elevator car collapsed. It was corroded. That's what the
article said. I just don't understand it.

He raises one eyebrow, in a sort of hook-shape. You'd think
the cable would have kept it in place, he says. You'd think
somebody would have noticed, anyway.

She purses her lips and nods, suddenly embarrassed, not
knowing what else to say.

Two kids, Donald says. His eyes remain on her face a moment too long.

It would be nice, she thinks, if I could turn this into a conversation about proper building maintenance, or about why it must be so hard to raise children in the city, or about Donald's background: did he grow up in a building with an elevator? Roger would have been able to. Roger was an expert at segues. *Speaking of Peru—Matt, you've been to Machu Picchu, haven't you?* But I, I, she thinks, am incapable of this. I've lost the ability to change the subject.

At her desk, she searches the New Jersey newspapers, and checks *El Diario* and *Hoy.* Nothing. You'd think it would be all over the news, splashed across the tabloids. But apparently children dying in strange ways isn't as newsworthy as it used to be. She spreads the *Times* across her desk and reads the article again, feeling blood seeping up her neck and across her cheeks.

Why?

Because it's one paragraph in the Metro Briefing section, she thinks, where they put the news that no one really cares about, and because if the paper hadn't flipped open in the breeze and my eyes happened to catch that tiny headline, and I hadn't stood there out of curiosity on the street with the dogwalkers and coffeedrinkers and strollerpushers dodging around me and read the whole story in ten seconds, I would never have known. The world sweats outrage: tragedy as filler, as background music. And this doesn't rate even a line? *Girls' Death Prompts Inquiry?* There are physical properties involved, for fuck's sake. Somebody should get to the bottom of it.

On impulse, she turns to her computer and types the names of the girls and the words *elevator accident* into Google.

Policereports.com
Dates, times, addresses
All reported events by community
100% guaranteed results $5.95.

So this is it, she thinks. Charity, in the end, is always faintly pornographic. Did Wilde say that? Well, so be it. She reaches under her desk for her wallet.

Her car, the last time she checked, was parked in a monthly outdoor lot on the other side of Broadway. Roger convinced her to put it there. Why park it on the street, he said, when you use it once a month, at most? He researched the options, and checked out each lot in turn, demanding references, negotiating for a better deal. And then, before she could stop him, he put the first six months on his platinum card. It's all part of the package, he said. Absurdly stingy, absurdly generous.

On her way down 67th Street she turns into a Duane Reade drugstore and wanders the aisles, wondering what she might be looking for. Birthday cards, wedding and graduation cards, engagements, births. Rosh Hashanah, Halloween, apologies, sympathy, regrets. A display of blue and pink teddy bears wearing tiny white t-shirts: *I ♥ NY—More Than Ever.* Should I buy one of those, she thinks, isn't that what you do these days? The store reeks of some floral perfume, as if they've poured it on the carpets. The merchandise seems distributed almost at random: shaving cream, laxatives, picture frames, men's magazines. Have the employees run away? she wonders. Did they abandon this sinking ship? Crossed the Williamsburg Bridge and the Holland Tunnel like rats down the gangplank?

Finally she sees the exit at the end of an aisle and hurries toward it, hardly able to stop from breaking into a run. White sunlight splashes her face, city sunlight, refracted by a hundred mirrored windows. Gratefully she breathes in exhaust and kebab smoke. What an American problem, she thinks, what to buy when nothing you can buy will make it any better, when no object makes any difference at all.

She hasn't driven in so long she's forgotten how fast it is, in the middle of the afternoon, crossing the Henry Hudson in a blur and swooping up the entrance ramp to the bridge, checking her watch—only five minutes have passed—putting both hands on the wheel to keep them from shaking, not looking over her shoulder, not even checking her rearview mirror, so as not to risk seeing the skyline, and in the space of that thought she's already arrived in New Jersey and is taking the exit for I-80, working on instinct, jabbing the buttons on the radio— a lilting Lester Young solo, a blizzard of Liszt, a calm voice reciting the names of accused terrorists in U.S. custody—and she hardly has time to look down at the driving instructions she printed out, remembering to take the second left after the exit ramp, onto Paterson Street, onto Wilkes Avenue, number 15, number 17, number 25.

A nondescript building at the corner of a busy block: seven stories, brick, with a rusting fire escape across the front. *Hampton Arms*, carved into a curved stone lintel above the door.

The ground floor houses a take-out restaurant that sells fried chicken and lake trout; even across the street, sitting inside her car, she smells hot oil and overcooked french fries. A group of teenagers passes her, happily shooting one another with enormous neon-yellow squirt guns.

There's only one Wilkes Avenue, she tells herself. There's only one number 25. She's left the motor running, the air conditioner blowing musty cold air against her knees. This is the building where it happened, and it doesn't matter that you're surprised to see no shreds of police tape in the street, no piles of wilted carnations, no candlewax dripped across the sidewalk, or photos bleaching in the sun. Who are you to show up after the fact with your editorializing, your pathetic expectations?

She gets out of the car anyway. and locks it twice to make sure. The late-afternoon sun seems to propel her across the street. A man comes out of the restaurant with a stained paper bag under his arm; a young woman carrying a baby pauses on the sidewalk and pulls a tissue from the pocket of her jeans. No one is watching her. The sunlight heavy as a velvet cape across her shoulders. She mounts the sidewalk and mounts the three stairs to the landing in front of the door, with crisp, measured steps, as if she's on an errand, and has a right to be there. Her pulse beats a frantic tempo in her wrists, in veins she didn't know she had. The old brass plate mounted on the wall next to the door has buttons and little windows where the names are supposed to be, but only one name is listed. *Figueroa. Apt 3B.*

She presses that button.

This is unacceptable, she thinks. You can't behave this way.

Behind the door, a jangling, clashing sound, as if someone is shaking an enormous ring of keys. The door swings open a foot, and a young woman's head appears, tilted sideways, as if she's determined to expose that much of herself and no more.

Sí? Que quiere?

Her face is heavily made up: foundation, rouge, lipstick the color of ripe plums. Bits of violet glitter around her eyes. Like someone you'd see in a video, Susan thinks, or a fashion ad. A professionally created face.

Perdoneme. It always happens this way, especially when she's rusty: in Spanish she speaks in a high, tremulous register, like a sixteen-year-old. Annoying, and utterly out of her control. *Pero aca está donde las niñas se murio la semana pasada?*

The woman's eyebrows—Susan hadn't noticed she *had* eyebrows—move together, like arrows meeting in midair.

Are you from Spain or something?

I'm American. But I studied in Madrid.

So you think I don't speak English, lady?

She swallows, her tongue dry as a sock.

What do you want, anyway? You a social worker? If you are, you're a little late. All those DYFS people came and went already, after the cops finished. You from the church?

I'm a translator, she says. A linguist. But that's not why I'm here. I'm just a private citizen. I read about what happened in the paper. I wanted to know if there's anything I could do to help.

Like what?

Well, she says, extemporizing, I'd like to set up a fund in

the girls' honor. For expenses. Maybe a scholarship. I'd like to make a donation.

It occurs to her, as soon as the words have left her lips, that she hasn't yet asked this person who she is.

I have to go to work in an hour. The woman lets the door swing open a few more inches. Below her throat, a name spelled out in rhinestones: *Cristina*. I guess you can come in for a few minutes, though, she says. A donation, you said? Come upstairs. *Viene.*

The elevator is in the middle of the hall, unavoidable, covered with two lengths of police tape in a haphazard X, the steel door battered and twisted half-open to the blackness of the shaft. She can't help turning toward it and staring.

The fire department really wrecked that thing, Cristina says. Tore it out with crowbars and then shoved it back in when they were done. That's how they had to get them out, through there. *Dios.* What a nightmare.

Are you related to them?

Martín is my boyfriend's cousin. They climb the stairs, Cristina's feet shuffling in flip-flops. Mexicans. Not like me. I'm old school Puerto Rican.

Are they here?

Nah. Nobody's here. I think they went to the funeral home again. The funeral's tomorrow. They had to delay it because of the autopsy.

She keeps climbing, putting one foot over another, though her joints feel as if they've been filled with something viscous and warm. Light streams into the stairwell from a dusty window. The air is stagnant, layered: pizza, fresh paint, something acrid, like burned brakes. At the third landing Cristina waves her through an open doorway into a small living room, neat, a sofa-and-loveseat set, an enormous silver TV, a glass coffee table piled high with stacks of jeans, boxer shorts, a mound of underwear in black and green and red.

I'm sorry, Susan says. She can't look at the clothes; it's a childish rigidity, the way she felt if Roger happened to see her in the bathroom. I'm disturbing you, she says. I'll just write the check and go. I shouldn't barge in this way.

What happened? Cristina waves at the couch. Sit down. I've got a few minutes. I mean, you're doing something *nice*. What am I, supposed to throw you out?

She disappears into the kitchen, leaving the question hanging in the air. Nothing to be done, Susan thinks, backing into the cushions, letting her weight down slowly, as if they might be stuffed with stones.

It's weird, you coming here today, Cristina says. The refrigerator thumps closed, ice clinking in glasses. I mean yesterday, the day before, the police were still down there investigating, the news truck came by twice. Though they never showed the story on TV. And we had all these people from the neighborhood coming through. Now it's just *quiet*. I woke up and a minute went by before I remembered it.

She comes back into the room, pushes the laundry aside, and puts two sweating glasses of iced tea on the table. Every movement accompanied by the silvery jangling of her bracelets, like the sound of sleighbells.

Did you know them well?

Her face takes on a strained inward attentiveness, as if she's working a loose tooth with her tongue. Sure, she says. I mean, we're family. Rita and Martín don't have PlayStation 2, so they were in and out of here all the time. We'd be shooing them out at ten so we could go to sleep, you know?

Susan allows herself a little half-nod, a dip of the head.

Micaela was the smart one. Cristina picks an ice cube out of her glass and rubs it against her forehead. Smart and chubby. She got a blue ribbon in the science fair. Her project was about sands and Africa, and how there's more desert all the time—

Desertification.

She wanted to be a biologist, that's what she said. A marine biologist. I said to her, listen, *gordita*, just don't grow up to tend bar and I'll be happy.

I was a waitress in college, Susan says. I barely lasted six months. After a shift I couldn't get out of bed till noon.

Yeah. It sucks. Cristina leans back on the sofa and smoothes out her jeans. But at the same time I'd never be happy sitting behind a desk all day. I got to be active. That's my personality. Moving, always moving.

They sit in silence, as if contemplating, she thinks, the lengths women will go to create the illusion of intimacy. A man would be in and out. Better yet, a card in the mail. A man, she thinks, any man, by which, not to generalize, I can only mean the men I've known, by which I mean Roger, would not attach himself like a leech, would not put himself at center stage, would not make it about *him, him, him.*

You said you're a translator, right?

A linguist. A book translator.

And you've never done this before? Counseling? Visiting

people? You're—I don't know. Kind of professional.

Maybe it's just my personality. She smiles, half in apology, half as a joke. When I lived in Veracruz one summer the guys there called me *blanca fria*.

Cristina manages a wan smile and scratches the corner of her mouth.

She takes a sip from her glass: strong tea, no sugar, just the way she would have made it, so cold it produces a pleasurable tightening at the back of her throat.

You're not married, are you? No kids?

She holds up her bare left hand.

I don't mean to be rude. I'm just talking.

It's OK, she says. Something about the apartment, how clean it is, how ordered, the spotless cream carpet, is making her feel, despite herself, almost relaxed. If I were in her position, she thinks, this is the kind of person I would *want* to be: calm, clear-headed, sensible. The underrated virtues. The ones not taught in graduate school.

I had five years with the same guy, she says. On and off. Her eyes wander across the opposite wall and come to rest on a window in the far corner of the room, its pale curtains drawn back, a steeple of blank blue sky. He died very suddenly. An aneurysm. No warning, no way to predict it. Painless, at least. It happened on the subway, on the way to the office.

The room's silence has a heavy, padded quality: all these soft forgiving surfaces. Cristina drapes a t-shirt across her knees and folds it without looking down. Imagination, you criminal, she thinks, my every weakness is yours. Crack the window and the apartment fills with soot. I shouldn't be let out in public.

What was the line from the movie? *You can't handle the truth.* That's me. I have no respect left for this world.

That's *terrible.* Cristina bites her lower lip. In a way it's worse than if you were married, isn't it? Because you can't say, *my husband died.* I mean, *my boyfriend?* It doesn't sound the same.

She says it factually, a simple observation, without condescension, or pity. And she's right, of course. If asked, Susan thinks, I would say exactly the same thing. But that doesn't stop the hot drill-bit of hatred boring through the bone between her eyes. For what, exactly? Saying the obvious?

Well, she says, brightly, it could be worse. We're still here. You have to believe that it's better to be a guilty survivor.

Cristina looks at her with a polite, lopsided smile.

I mean, you weren't in the elevator with them. You have to be grateful for that.

But if I'd been there it wouldn't have happened.

The pressure shifts now to her temples, and she feels herself wincing, as if her head is trapped in a vise.

Why, she hears herself asking. I don't get it. Why?

It's not like it was an accident. The girls were playing in there. They got hold of something sticking out and the whole thing was rusted and it just came down on them.

The paper didn't say anything about that.

Who cares what the papers said?

She can feel the metal grips of the vise, its little teeth, smashing the papery skin behind her eyes. Tiny fireworks erupt at the edges of her field of vision. She reaches out for the glass and nudges it off the edge of the table, and it lands with a soft thump, spilling a blot of tea across the carpet. Jesus. She stands up, but Cristina has already returned from the kitchen with a roll of paper towels. I'm so clumsy! she says. Shit. I'm sorry.

Martín had nothing to do with it, Cristina says, tearing sections of towel and spreading them out across the stain. She angles her head upward to catch Susan's eye. It was all painted over, and nobody had checked for the rust underneath. The inspector must have been paid off or something. We just moved in here a year ago. I mean, of course they should have known better, right? But it wasn't their fault. Kids do stupid things. You can't account for it.

Though at the same time, Susan says, you know what caused it. It isn't as if it came down out of the blue. It was preventable. Theoretically. You don't have to ask yourself, *Why wasn't I there instead?* You see what I mean?

Cristina sits up on her haunches and surveys the damage, sucking her pursed lips. Yeah, she says. *Theoretically* it makes a difference. But no matter what you have to go on with your life, don't you? Martín was saying they're going to start trying for another baby right away.

Children die, she thinks. They climb onto junkpiles and get stuck in old refrigerators; they flip over the handlebars with no helmet on; they get struck by garbage trucks on the way to school. And the parents, somehow, always recover, don't they? They have more babies; they adopt. Life fills those voids. How could it not? How would the species survive?

You have to stop looking, she thinks. You have to stop lying your way into the right metaphor. Nothing works by analogy anymore. The act of comparing is another kind of violence.

She reaches into her bag and finds her checkbook.

Listen, she says, flipping open the cover, I should be going. But I want to leave something for the family. She writes the date, and his name, and quickly scratches a 1 in the box, followed by four zeros. *Ten thousand dollars exact*, she writes across the line below, in her slanting precise hand. She has a little more than that in her savings, but not much. *To cash*, she writes on the back.

It's Roger's money, most of it, she thinks. All the bills he paid, sometimes without telling her; the dinners and taxi rides and vacations.

She folds the check in half and hands it to Cristina, who turns it over, as if there's something written on the other side, opens it, and reads it, expressionless.

You don't want to leave a note or something?

What could I say, she wonders. Put it in a college fund. Save up for a down payment on a house with stairs. What can I tell him that he doesn't already know? Who made me an authority on the future?

On the interstate, heading east, she follows one sign after another for New York, switching lanes, using her signal, trying to stay in the correct arrow-path. *Paramus. Lodi. The Oranges. Hackensack.* The highway floats above them, on a cushion of green; all she sees are rooftops, gas station signs, billboards she doesn't have to time to read. The highway divides and subdivides: Upper Level or Lower Level? Cash or EZ-Pass? Whatever that is, she thinks, I don't have it. I don't have an EZ-anything. She moves over to the right, twice, and joins a long line of cars inching toward the toll plaza.

Nobody ever gets lost, her great-aunt Margaret said, over a plateful of potato salad at the family Fourth of July barbeque in Woods Hole. She was telling a story about a woman she'd known forty years earlier, when they were both young brides-to-be in Boston. The woman turned out to be living two doors down from their new condominium in Delray Beach. It's as if it was yesterday, Margaret said. We didn't need to explain anything at all.

Everyone was going to great lengths not to make her feel self-conscious, Susan finally decided; that was the most chari-table explanation. It was all a little scripted, the total absence of drawn-out hugs, of *Oh, Susan, how have things been since—*. No tortuous conversations in the kitchen with the cousins. I don't want to be a spectacle, she'd told her mother, I don't want to be an example of what could happen. This isn't 1955. But when Margaret said those four words, a truism she'd never known to exist, like a strange Finnish proverb, she thought, I could use a little self-consciousness here. *I could use a little pity.*

Nobody ever gets lost: was it like that law of physics she'd learned in high school, matter cannot be created or destroyed, only changed in form? If so, she wanted to ask, then where is he? Where is Roger, specifically? In a clutch of goldenrod by the side of the interstate in Iowa? A cat sunning itself on a roof in Berlin?

It wouldn't be fair, she finally decided, to expect them to realize that despite its seeming surface continuity, the world's underlying chemistry had been permanently altered. It would be like telling them that L.L.Bean was run by Republicans:

true, but beside the point. Somebody has to remain innocent, she thought, in the café car coming back through Connecticut, toasting her escape from New England, as she always did, with a miniature bottle of Chardonnay. Somebody has to remain uncorrupted by viciousness and random horror. As if the things we clung to are still sufficient: freshly mown lawns, Great-grandmother's damask tablecloths, the framed letter from Robert Kennedy at the top of the stairs. As if they were still alive, as if they still mattered. As if we still mattered.

As she leaves the toll booth and pulls toward the right lane the traffic gains momentum, and the great cables of the bridge rise up on either side, like giant wings, like Gothic arches. She thinks, *This is my cathedral.* She rolls the windows down, and hot, sticky air rushes through the car, smelling of the river. Roger, she thinks, if I had your ashes I would carry them out to the middle in a Chinese takeout container, and toss them off, just casually, over my shoulder. Roger, if you could have died the way you lived, with sarcasm, with subtlety, with the Pixies on the stereo, then it would have been all right. If it had been AIDS, if it had been *leukemia*, it would have been okay, as long as we had twenty-four hours' notice, enough time to call a few friends and chill a bottle of champagne, so we could drink it at the bitter end, like Chekhov.

If you had stopped at Starbucks.

If you had lingered on the 1 reading the paper instead of taking the 2.

If you had thought it was OK to show up at work *thirty seconds late.*

If you had stopped to talk to Rachel Abramowitz, who passed you on the platform at 7:49, your college friend, whom you hadn't seen in years, instead of saying, Sorry, I've got to rush, *give me a call*, and handing her your card.

If numbers hadn't been invented.

If God hadn't been invented.

If the word *because* hadn't been invented.

If the word *therefore* hadn't been invented,

If we understood what words meant in the first place,

Then you wouldn't have been reduced to a puff of smoke, a vague and unpleasant *smell*, not a shard, not a fleck of skin or blood, you wouldn't have been sterilized out of existence by a ten-thousand-degree fire, and I wouldn't be flying across this bridge with my mouth open, as if I could eat the air. She turns her head, now halfway across, and looks down the whole length of the island, through the gray-gold haze, searching for the gap. How is it, she wonders, that you're supposed to find something that isn't there? The pages don't turn backward. There's no word for that kind of love, in this language or any other.

The Call of Blood

Mornings he finds Mrs. Kang upright in bed, peeling invisible ginger with an invisible knife. She watches her hands with rapt attention, picking up the stalks from a pile at her right and dropping the peeled pieces into a bowl on her lap. A cloud of white hair rises from her scalp, fine as spun sugar. The first time he tries to raise her, putting his hands gently beneath her armpits, she bats them away; the second time she forgets to resist. She weighs eighty-eight pounds on a good day. In the wheelchair she sits up, ramrod-straight, and waves a finger at him. *Kaesul hun'bok chasaeoh!* Her voice like wind in a crevasse. You are a bad boy!

Hyunjee, her daughter, says, No offense, Kevin. But if she knew it was a black man taking care of her, it would finish her off.

She has a funny way of smiling, like squinting into the sun. He can tell she finds this thought faintly entertaining.

I'm not *black*, he says. My father was from Jamaica and my mother was from Queens. Irish Queens.

Oh, I know, she says. It's complicated. But it wasn't complicated for her. She was held up three times. After Dad died and she was trying to run the place alone. She had nightmares for years afterwards. Wouldn't admit it, though. Typical Korean mother.

Hyunjee's hair is already streaked gray on one side, though she can't be much older than forty. She wears it long with a wooden clasp, and loose-cut linen clothes, all in blues and browns and blacks. A jewelry maker—he has her card—who doesn't wear any herself. Divorced, with two little girls who come only once every two weeks or so. She comes every day, with food in a stack of steel boxes.

She was saying something different today, he says. Something like *Dung gum kuel go chora.*

Dum gum kuel go chora. Scratch my back.

Okay. I'll remember that.

You don't have to do everything she says, you know.

If she's itchy it means that her skin is too dry, he says. It could be a sign of dermatitis. That's what you're paying me for, to watch out for those things. The hospital nurses won't do it.

He shifts his weight from one leg to the other, trying to relieve the bone-ache in his arches, but nothing helps. These Nikes are two weeks old; he's tried lacing them loose, tight, in-between. There's no stepping out of the shadow of this pain.

It's too bad, she says, her back to him, shoveling leftovers into the garbage, filling the room with the smell of sour cabbage and garlic. Until last year her English wasn't bad. She used to watch Oprah every day. But after she woke up from the stroke—nothing. What a shame, you know? All that wasted effort.

Not wasted. She used it to survive.

She used to say speaking English made her tongue tired. And it's true! Even I remember that, from when I was first learning. All the correct sounds in Korean are wrong in English. It's absurd, really, if you think about it. Nobody should have to work that hard to ask for a glass of water.

Count yourself lucky, he thinks, that she can speak at all.

He could tell her about the saddest cases, the old women with half-melted faces, their minds wiped clean by a clot smaller than a baby's fingernail. But nurses don't compare. To do so would be to suggest this patient is not the only patient in the universe, their only and every and always, their one sole concern. Doctors, yes. Doctors comfort by comparing, by giving the odds. Nurses never say, *it could be worse.*

His mother, on the other hand, never lost her gift for languages, right up to the end. Fluent in Latin and French by seventeen, thanks to the Carmelite Sisters of Charity, she took up patois with the steely determination of a missionary. His father's parents, so the story went, refused to believe that the woman they'd spoken to on the phone was white until she stepped onto the tarmac in Kingston shielding herself from the sun with a blue parasol. Years after his father died she stayed a part-time community liason for Catholic Social Services, who could be contacted by phone at a moment's notice, and it wasn't unusual, when he was in high school, to come home and find her at the kitchen table, sorting the bills, the phone clasped between shoulder and chin, her face the color of boiled lobster, saying, *y'cyaan stay wid dat man, soon as 'im get money 'im gone.*

It embarrassed him, in a small, private way. He himself could understand his Jamaican relatives only barely and not speak it at all. Like the taste of ackee and jerk chicken: a foreign thing colored by the guilt of having once been familiar. At fourteen he had refused to go to his father's sister's Christmas party in Flatbush, claiming he was no longer a Christian, and somehow that single gesture, that flutter of adolescent pique, had poisoned the well. No more presents, not even a birthday card. Tell them, he told his mother finally, years later, tell them I'm not ashamed to be part Jamaican, that's not it, I meant no harm. I was just a kid. She looked at him over the rim of her coffee mug and said, well, you *meant* no harm. That must be some consolation.

When his mother died, his father's family held a Nine Night ceremony after the Mass and didn't invite him. He was twenty-one, two weeks off the plane from Saudi Arabia, desperate for a pair of flabby arms and a perfumed shoulder, a mouthful of curry goat. Instead he stumbled home from the Liffey at 3 a.m. Two days later he was on the graveyard shift at St. Vincent's, picking buckshot from a gangbanger's backside. Like the grunts always said: when you get off the plane, go down on your knees and kiss the ground. Tunnel into it like an earthworm. Don't make any serious decisions for the first six months. He was lucky, having never fired a shot, flipped a switch, thrown a grenade, he could carry on the same work with no interruption, one war zone to another. Like switching saline bags on an IV. A continuous flow of tears.

Sometimes he feels his brain curdling. *Curdling*: exactly the word for it. A snatch of conversation in the elevator, the head-lines on Hyunjee's copy of the *Times*, a few bars of a song someone whistles in the bathroom: always it takes him a moment too long to see the point, to put words to the melody. Synapses atrophy, lose their shape, their elasticity, their charge. Why should he be surprised? An hour spent folding towels, testing bath water, dividing pills into groups for the night nurses: not a single abstract thought. Even the taking of vital signs boils down to a series of small muscle movements: tightening the velcro, flicking off the old thermometer cup, squeezing the wrist with two fingers, just so. The brain carries the numbers as long as it takes to insert a quarter into a vending machine. The body drones on, he thinks, the autonomous nervous system taking care of itself quite nicely with the cerebral cortex switched off.

Have you been a nurse for a long time? Hyunjee asks, her back turned, watering the row of potted plants on the windowsill.

Since 1989, on and off.

Is that the proper word to use? I'm not up on the terminology.

If there was another term for it, it wouldn't matter. A nurse is a nurse.

You don't seem old enough to have been working in 1989.

I joined the Army when I was eighteen. I was a medic in the Gulf War.

Oh.

He can hear her thoughts recalibrating, one assumption leapfrogging backward over another. It's okay, he wants to tell her, no one ever believes it. That certain slackness in the way he moves, as if he was all double-jointed, Renée called it. Hard to imagine him in formation with the helmet and the gun. His mother used to say, What is it about you that always finds the farther corner in the room?

I thought medics were doctors.

Medics are just grunts with a little bit of extra training. The MDs work in the field hospitals, out of sight, way back from the front lines.

She sticks a finger into the soil of each pot before and after watering, frowning, as if the perfect dampness is hard to achieve. A large hydrangea, the color of barely boiled tea, two long trailing ivy plants, a kind of small shrub with tiny, waxy leaves. He's never seen anyone look after plants so intently. What is her house like? he permits himself to wonder. Pristine, presumably. No dust bunnies in the corners. All uniform colors. Lots of wood, no clutter. Elaborate cabinetry. Hidden richness on all sides.

And how long did you stay in the Army?

Not long. Discharged in '92.

She's brought him a stack of forms to fill out from the insurance company, a whole Conditions of Care portfolio and six-month review. Most of it she could fill in herself. Not that he would point that out to her in so many words. That's not the way a private nurse keeps clients, especially the guilty ones, the ones who want to feel like they're doing everything they can. Still, he has to grit his teeth now and then, turning a page to see another row of boxes waiting for the near-puncturing tip of his pen. Little black flashes of rage at her helplessness.

Unacceptable, he tells himself, inappropriate, ridiculous. I'm a fucking thesaurus these days.

My feet are freezing. She speaks to the window, to no one in particular. The puddles on Second Avenue are fifteen feet across. I always mean to buy a new pair of boots and never get around to it.

I can get you a pair of hospital slippers if you want.

Her laugh is high and piping and uncharacteristically girlish.

Thanks. I'm not *that* desperate.

Some indefinite tension lingers in the air. As if it's a joke and he guessed the punchline by accident too soon. So it is with me, he thinks, never one for chitchat.

I've been meaning to ask you something, she says. And I want you to give me a frank answer. I should have her at home, shouldn't I? I mean, medically speaking, there's nothing keeping her here, right? It's not as if I don't have the space. The girls can bunk up again. You just have to say the word—

You'd have to pay me almost double. Plus a night nurse. Rentals, too. Home dialysis equipment, a hospital bed, a wheelchair, plus all the supplies. It would mean turning your house into a miniature clinic. Plus trips back here when she gets an infection or has to change her stent.

All that's required? I mean, like by law or something?

At moments like these her face drains of expression, a strange placidity, the opposite, he thinks, of real calm, of actual relaxation. Without looking back she reaches behind her and touches the old woman's foot, the tender ankle with its close webwork of veins.

It's the standard of care.

Her village in Korea didn't get electricity till the eighties, she says. Her father dug the family well by hand. She grew up eating meat once a week if she was lucky.

Then she's one of the fortunate ones.

I don't know if that's what she'd call it.

Good thing there's no choice in the matter.

These are the kind that just *go*, a resident said to him, once, in a low voice, when they were alone in the room. You could turn around and the hematode simplex is dissecting and you'd never know. A hundred things depend on her saying *right* and *left*. Fucking Alzheimers. You might as well be back with the dogfish in Gross Anatomy. She's a regular time bomb, this one. But I don't have to tell you that.

He fixed him with a look. Why, he said. Why don't you have to tell me that.

You went to med school. I can tell. Your notes are too detailed.

I guess that's a compliment.

Well, then, you *should* have gone to med school.

He muttered under his breath.

Quae vero inter curandum, aut Etinam Medicinam, minime faciens, in communi hominum vita, vel videro, vel audiero, quae minime in vulgus esseri oportear, ca arcana esse ratus, filebo.

What's that?

What I may see or hear in the course of the treatment or even outside of the treatment in regard to the life of men, which on no account one must spread abroad, I will keep to myself, holding such things shameful to be spoken about.

Damn.

My sergeant was kind of a sadist. Made us memorize it before we could run an IV.

Seriously, though. Was it the money?

He's a healthy, six-foot-two Indian kid with long, tapering fingers, trying to make himself older with thin gold wire-loop glasses and a rep tie. From one of those leafy Midwestern suburbs, Shaker Heights or Grosse Pointe. A certain guilelessness, the product of a vigorous uncynical public-school upbringing. Doctor and Doctor Sharma with the matching Mercedes. Work as a nurse in New York long enough, he thinks, and you'll meet everyone: the upwardly mobile, the failing fast, and the stick-it-outs, the in-betweens, too perverse or lazy to be counted.

Yeah. Somehow my fairy godmother never came along.

Well, you never know, right? There's loans. You're still young.

Listen, he says, I *like* nursing. Want to know why? Because it's women's work.

Dr. Sharma draws in his shoulders, protectively, and blinks.

Seriously, he says. Look at her. Nothing to be done, right? Tacrine, donepezil—they ran through that years ago. Vitamin E supplements? And then a whole slew of antidepressants. She was diagnosed as ALZ-likely twenty years ago and ever since it's been a comedy of fucking errors. One doctor coming in after another and trying to fix it. That's not how it works, man. Pay attention to the basic science! Until they find every single one of those triggers in the DNA and figure out how to turn them off, all anyone's going to be able to do is be there day by day, trying to keep those synapses exercised. You have to sit there and try until there's no point anymore. And you're *going* to fail. That's the difference right there. Doctors hate nothing more than a certain failure. But for nurses, man, that's life. That's *medicine*.

Look, Sharma says. I get it. It's not just changing bedpans. I just can't see living in New York on a nurse's salary.

You just have to travel light. No kids, no encumbrances. I'm not looking for a condo on the Bowery.

I was thinking more like a three bedroom in Flushing.

What, he wants to ask, is it sympathy for doctors day? You mean I'm not the only martyr in the building? Well, he says, it's a sad world when a young M.D. can't make a mortgage payment.

Yeah. Businesslike, now, his pride wounded, he knocks Mrs. Kang's chart with two knuckles, and lets it clatter back into its holder at the foot of the bed. I should get back to my rounds, he says.

Buck up, though, he calls after him. Once you're past the Boards you can give out Botox injections on the side.

It's not about the body, he's thinking, and not *not* about the body. Her clothes are loose, squared-off, raw silk, unbleached cotton, cashmere. Drapery. They generalize her figure. Only when she squats or reaches or bends low does he become aware of the generosity of her hips, the smooth unfreckled cleft of her breasts. She never arouses him, not in person, not in daydreams. Nothing as obvious as that. *Her smoldering frustration.* Like her scent, not perfume, not soap, but there in the room nonetheless, slightly sweet and damp.

So unlike the clatter and innuendo outside in the corridor. Men can't resist a woman in scrubs, even the ugliest mismatched laundry-room rejects; he certainly never could. That was the one benefit of switching to paramedic, in the days after Renée, or, to be honest, during and after: the whole parade of them, doe-eyed fresh RN's, lacy bras and thongs underneath, in spare rooms, in supply closets, in his bed at 4 a.m. after a shift and an hour slamming beers. It's the oldest feeling in the world, or the second-oldest, after just plain lust. Survivor's guilt. Like all the stockbrokers shacking up after the towers fell. Terror sex, they called it, but it had nothing to do with terror. You look at pain, you gape at it, and then tear yourself away and eat Froot Loops. Pure instinct. A shift of heart attacks and GSW's and eight-year-old girls with fingers burned off in the toaster and what else could you possibly want? A candy bar, a shot of Jameson, a bacon double cheeseburger, and your face buried in Nicole Scangarello's pussy in the backseat of her Altima pulled over at a rest stop on the way out to Huntington Beach.

He was never particular in those days. You took what came. Hospitals, again: a great equalizer. Sponsor of thousands of mongrel births. He never understood the guys who swore by Bronx Dominicans or Flatbush Chinese or Staten Island Italians. And the girls: were they aroused by his blackness? Not likely. Not that he ever knew. His body was never so remarkable as to engender much comment. It was a body, it was available, it was alive; that was the coin of the realm. He doesn't miss the sex so much, the messiness of all that grappling, all those unfamiliar shapes beneath the fingers, the odd discoveries, pounding away to get the nut no matter if the sweetness is gone, but he misses the reassurance. And misses being awake so often in the hour of necessity, the hot glare of the streetlights just before dawn.

Hyunjee has his home number. Not just his cell, his business number, which he turns to silent on weekends and the evenings—a substitute for his old answering service—but the old black rotary phone that just rings: no answering machine, no caller ID, no volume control, not even a plug to unhook from the wall. He gave it to her the first day her mother was admitted; it was something about the hapless way she fell into the chair in the waiting room and curled her legs to one side. New Yorkers don't act that way when engaging a service signing a contract. It unnerved him when he showed her the payment schedule and she barely glanced it over. He flipped over his card and scrawled the number across the back. I'll always be at one of these, he said. Don't worry.

Now he checks his cell messages on a Sunday morning, no less. In case she's too shy to *bother him at home*. Sweaty, after running, peeling off his shirt and nylon jacket, draping a towel around his shoulders. The way she molds the dirt into little mounds with her fingertips. Her deftness with the metal chopsticks that never click against the side of the bowl. I could use a little pruning. A stupid way to put it. A woman's face creased with quiet anxiety. *Care*, he thinks, I could use someone else's care. I've grown too good at it myself.

Watch yourself, now. As if the world needed a whole new

dimension of tired and pathetic. You'd have to wait till after the old woman died, and then what? A phone call two weeks after the funeral? *I thought we might have dinner?*

You can't afford it, he thinks, there comes a point in life when every investment is a loss, every additional effort is a mistake. Do yourself a favor. Do yourself a service. The luxury of not waiting out another six months of heartache. He steps into the plastic stall with its long skid mark of rust running from the faucet to the drain, thinking, do something about that, if you want to do something. And leaves the water on cold for a moment longer than usual, till his teeth are chattering.

When he walked into the classroom on the first day of Korean 110 the teacher covered her mouth, to cover a laugh, or a grimace of horror, perhaps some new fusion of the two she'd never before imagined. He wedged himself into a chair between Katrina Lee and Jenny Park and tried his best to follow her explanation of *hangul*, an jumble of little circles and boxes and stick-figure men.

It's a very difficult language, she said to him afterwards. Even for them—she indicated the young Korean-American women vanishing through the door, zipping backpacks. flipping open their mobile phones. They grow up hearing it and still it takes them years. What makes you interested in learning it?

I have a Korean girlfriend.

He'd been flipping through the course catalog on the toilet—it came in the mail, unbidden, three times a year—meditating on the question of other possible lives. Introduction to Reiki. Advanced Flavors of the Mediterranean. Systems Analysis and the Diversified Portfolio. The listing for the introductory language classes said, *no previous experience necessary, for the absolute beginner.* He liked that phrase, its wishful absurdity. As if there was any such thing as an absolute beginner.

Then she can teach you, yes?

She's shy. Anyway, she doesn't have enough time. I want to learn it properly, from the ground up. Her parents don't speak English.

She crossed her arms and gave a broad, worldly laugh. That's very well-intentioned of you, she said. But the problem might not be the language barrier.

Am I making you uncomfortable? he was tempted to say. She didn't even bother to disguise the way she moved behind the desk when he came near. Uninhibited fear and discomfort: what a revelation! You could almost respect her for it.

Well, it's my money, he said.

It amazes him, now, three months gone, the term nearly finished. Every word he speaks out loud sending ripples of wincing distaste through the room. Teacher Cho has perfected the art of derision by example. *Bol*, she says, flapping her tongue at him, to demonstrate the way it had to be placed: curled behind the teeth, a little coiled snake. Not *bowl. Bol.* Long after he's gotten it right. *That's you,* Renée used to say, *stubborn as a rock when you've made up your mind.* Meant not entirely as praise. But mostly.

Mul jum kajigo wara, Mrs. Kang says.

I want some water.

Mul jum kajigo wara.

A sentence flowing at him out of a dream. He stands by the window, scrubbing iodine off the toe of his sneaker, he wipes his fingers on a paper towel, and inches his neck around until his head rotates half the distance between them.

Cham gam manyo, mul kajoda deureul gayo? he asks.

Mul kajoda.

Her eyes shift in his direction: wet drops of onyx, bright as always, brighter than seeing eyes can ever be. Who does she think is speaking, he wonders. She stretches out a palsied finger, pointing at the bathroom door. A tap. A pump. A well. Eventually the disease squeezes out every memory, he knows that, even the earliest: the bottle, the mother's breast. But right now, who am I to her? Son, father, uncle, nurse, servant?

Mul kajoda. He catches himself saying it. The tip of the tongue placed exactly in the middle of the palate. *Mul. Mul.*

And here you thought it would never happen, he thinks. You thought it would never click. All that wasted time.

Kevin—

Hyunjee in the doorway, looking from one face to another, her face saying, *If there was one thing I understood in this world, it's gone now.*

He's forgotten the daughters. Their names, their ages, the particular blur of each face. The taller of the two full-grown, shoulder-high on him, the other some indeterminate late-childhood shape, all bright wholesome fabrics and plastic beads. They're uptown for the weekend with their father, but he's thinking, as they walk up Second Avenue from the Thai restaurant back toward her apartment, that he should have something to say on the general subject of children, why he and Renée never had any, the difficulties of being a single mother—being a child of one—the hardships of the New York City schools. A certain widening of the circle of the conversation. He needs to bring things up to date, to gesture toward the immediate past, the impending future. Amy, Elizabeth, Lisa, Allison? Nondescript, easy names, names indicative of compromise, of shying away from the fashionable, not making things more difficult than they would already be.

Though one could hardly say she's given him much of an opening. Come get a bite with me tomorrow, was all she said. Stanley's got the girls for the weekend. I could use some adult conversation. This whole you-studying-Korean thing—she waved her hand, as if to say, *I don't get it, I don't* have *to get it.* I mean, she said, it's strange, isn't it, spending so much time together, never actually getting to know each other? Maybe to you it's not. But you don't have to come if you don't want to. Strictly optional.

And now he's lightheaded, pathetic dateless creature, swinging along the sidewalk as if he owns Manhattan, free-associating through the past, a tour of sedimented longings he hasn't unearthed in years.

Strange to think now that a poem could cause so much fuss. But that's what happens when you get married at twenty-three, married out of sheer desperation, before you're relieved of the burden of having to plot your life like a drama on TV. It was the one thing he took from four years of high school English; he chose it at random out of the textbook when the assignment was to memorize and recite to the class.

It is well, my child, that you never traveled
The long, long way that begins with school days
When little fingers blur under the tears
That fall on the crooked letters
And the earliest wound, when a little mate
leaves you alone for another;

Tell me a poem, Renée had asked him one night, when they were three or four months married. Say a poem for me. You always reading, you've got to know at least one. It was July, no A/C in the apartment, thin plasticky sheets from the dollar store, and he must have been pissed, anyway, as he almost always in those days, having to come inside after the fourth beer out on the stoop. Pissed, full of a young man's useless bile, whatever, there was no excuse.

And sickness; and the face of fear by the bed;
The death of a father or mother;
Or shame for them, or poverty;
The maiden sorrow of school days ended;
And eyeless Nature that makes you drink
From the cup of Love, though you know it's poisoned;

Flat on his back, the sheets girded around his waist, and her on her side, facing him, cupping her head with her hand. Her girlish nakedness, the high breasts, slender arms, the sheen of sweat on her forehead.

To whom would your flower-face have been lifted?
Botanist, weakling? Cry of what blood to yours?
Pure or foul, for it makes no matter,
It's blood that calls to our blood.
And then your children—oh, what might they be?
And what your sorrow? Child! Child!
Death is better than Life!

He spoke the last lines in a cold sweat, recalling and understanding them all at once, unable to stop, enjoying it a little
bit too. The way Mrs. Gombromowicz's face took on color
and lost it, the way she sat alert at her desk. Yo, that shit is
cold, someone muttered. A perfect seventeen-year-old's Fuck
You to the world. Renée turned her back to him and pulled
the sheet around her shoulders. When she finally consented
to speak to him again, three days later, she said, *I get it. I get
you now,* and refused even to hear the apology he'd composed.
That was love, he guessed. And she gave herself to him no
less fervently than before, but became rigid and mathemati-
cal about birth control, the pills and creams and the rubbers
whenever she might have missed a day or just when she felt, as
she often felt, *vulnerable.*

Pure or foul, for it makes no matter. Hard to believe, now, that it
could be that simple. Those were the days. My excesses, he
thinks, all of the emotional kind, these ludicrous blind gestures, the kind you can't take back. Having years to burn. And
we burned them, too.

There's something I meant to ask you about, she says, after
they've walked a block in silence. Next week's her birthday. I

was wondering if it would be appropriate to celebrate. In the room, I mean.

He wonders if he should be annoyed; business on a date, isn't that one of those basic rules? Instead he opts for generosity, a light laugh. Of course, you should do anything you want. She's not in a coma, you know. Anything she recognizes helps.

It's also her wedding anniversary.

All the better. A tape recording of your father, maybe? Or a piece of his clothing.

And a bottle of soju. She used to drink herself silly and talk to his picture, every year. Stories from her village. I should have used a tape recorder. Is there some rule against getting the patients drunk?

He laughs so loudly passerby look up from their conversations, startled. She doesn't need it, he says. That's the good side of Alzheimers. You're permanently blotto.

She opens the door, drops her keys in a glass bowl in the hallway, opens the refrigerator, and carries a bottle and two glasses across the living room to the sliding door of the balcony, without looking at him, without asking permission. Shucking her mules absentmindedly halfway across the carpet. A chrome-and-glass coffee table, a pair of black leather couches, an Eames chair, enormous plastic-looking ferns. *His* furniture. Everything you can't afford to replace in a divorce, and the kids want it, anyway, no matter how horrible, it's what they've grown into, and the continuity matters.

I'm curious about something, she declares, and I want to be honest about it. No pussyfooting around. I want to know what it was like over there.

It wasn't even a real war. Not like the one they're in now.

That's a poor excuse for an answer.

I'll tell you this much, he says. Sand gets into everything. I had this expensive camera, a Nikon, and it was trashed by the time I left. Sand driven through the seal into the lens. It sticks to your skin. The slightest bit of moisture makes it stick. You get so that it sticks to your dick and keeps you from jerking off.

The wine has a cloying floral bouquet, like sweet perfume; he licks his lips trying to get rid of it. Half my high school signed up, he says. Four tables right outside the main doors starting in April. Like shooting fish in a barrel. They took the kids who graduated two or three years ahead of us, the ones we looked up to, and sent them back as recruiters. It was a god-damned reunion out there every day. Gave them nice watches, good insurance policies, anything they could show off.

So you were manipulated into it.

I was looking for another father. A certain perverted kind of unconditional love. And instead what you get is Daddy slapping you across the face every other minute.

I understand that.

No you don't, he wants to say, quickly, a splash of cold water across the eyes. But says, instead, it wasn't for me. Some really get into the camaraderie aspect, the brotherhood. It feels good to be needed when you're that age. And, you know, it teaches you to get your shit together. Get up and take a shower in the morning, no complaining. It's a *job*. They say it's the best and worst training for the rest of your life.

He chuckles.

As long as we're on unpleasant topics—

He's a lawyer. You might have heard his name. Stanley Pollack. Civil rights stuff, mainly, First Amendment issues. Whistleblower cases. Pretty high profile. He's a commentator on WNYC.

Does that bother you?

What, hearing his voice? Come on. We're on the phone two or three times a week anyway. He's a pretty involved father. Or at least he talks a good game. The divorce was amicable, in the end, I guess. We used a mediator. No betrayals, no infidelities. That I know of, anyway. Just pain. Ordinary, exhausting, unglamorous pain. We married too young; we got tired. You know the one about the wooden peg in the table?

You mean the round peg in the square hole.

No, no. Say you've got a wooden peg stuck in a table and you want to get it out. The only way is to bang in another peg. You're always back where you started, in other words.

So you throw away the table.

Something like that. I was never good at analogies.

And the girls?

The girls are over there having a grand old time. Takeout sushi and movies on cable till 3 a.m. if they want. He lets them watch *Sex and the City* and they come home talking about cocaine and anal sex. The only rule is they can't leave the apartment. Stan's a paranoid old New Yorker. Still won't walk through Central Park at night.

He'll have a hard time when they get older.

They *are* older. Samantha's having her bat mitzvah in October.

Is that right, he says. Trying to connect the word with a particular age. Is it like confirmation, he wonders, or like a sweet sixteen? Or neither.

I converted before we were married. Not that we ever went to synagogue. But the bat mitzvah's non-negotiable. His parents are footing the bill.

Underneath her cardigan is a flimsy silk tank-top, almost the top of a nightgown. Off comes the sweater, wadded up in her lap. He's surprised by the broadness of her shoulders. Not unlike Renée's, in truth. Who was a pole vaulter, All-Queens Track. On a long thin chain she wears a flat gold disk the size of a nickel, polished, catching the light. He reaches and turns it between his fingers. No markings on either side. Like a slug for busting old Coke machines, a penny on the railroad tracks, burned smooth.

That a piece of yours?

She swallows the last of her wine and pours another glass.

We could sit here and ask each other questions all night, she says. We could get to know each other incredibly well in a couple of hours. Is that what you want?

But there is one more story, the one he tells her in the smearing blue light of six-thirty, before his shift begins and he becomes her employee again. Renée's last day in the apartment. He was just home from work, and heard her moving around in the bedroom, talking on the phone, so he'd think it was her mother and would pick up the line in the kitchen. That was their strange habit, these party-line calls, because Shirley loved him—more than her own daughter, Renée always claimed—and would always be clamoring for him to get on the phone. She lived in South Carolina, a good place to raise children, she always reminded them, better than the snowy wastes of Hollis.

It wasn't Shirley, of course. It was a man's voice, grinning at her across the line, making her giggle. Baby, I *know* you want me to get it out! it said. I *know* you can't stand waiting another minute! But I'm gonna *make* you wait! He dropped the receiver into its cradle as if it was white smoking iron and stared straight ahead. A head of cabbage, an ice tray left out on the counter to melt. His own keys, left casually in the bowl next to the door. The simplest objects had a way of betraying you: all the unpredictable meanings they took on. He stared at each one, each *thing*, making an inventory, before walking out the door.

Only later did he realize he was waiting for her to come out of the bedroom and explain.

They run into each other now, every so often, when he's back visiting a friend in the neighborhood. She held onto the apartment but not the man, Rodney or Rudolph or Randolph, even after she bore him the son he claimed he wanted more than anything, more than a winning lottery ticket or a house in Barbados. A daughter and two sons. Her mother lives across the street now, he's heard. Whenever he sees her he feels as if they're meeting in a garden, a lawn hedged with bright flowers, or a patio with a fountain in the middle. An absolute and unshakeable peace. As if one pain canceled out another.

There's a special place in hell reserved for people like that, Hyunjee says, rolling onto her back and dropping her fingers lightly against his thigh. Betrayal by telephone is in a category all by itself.

I stopped blaming her a long time ago.

Cosmic retribution, though. That you can hope for.

No, he says, that's not my life. That's not a way to live.

If it had been me I would've been cured of sex for good.

Maybe I am.

Don't say things like that, she says. I hate repartée. It's boring. Not when I can still feel you inside me. You haven't been cured of anything. Thank god.

All right, then. Have it your way.

I would have wanted those years of my life back. Presumably that's why I'm still alone. My capacity for forgiveness is too low.

Is that a warning?

Immediately he wishes he'd stopped up his mouth, sucked in a wad of cotton, a roll of toilet paper. Even a brick would've done, in a pinch.

It might be, she says. Would you like it to be?

She's beginning to refuse food. When Hyunjee lifts the lid and releases the smell of *kalbi* into the room her eyes pucker in alertness and fear. *My teeth hurt,* she says. *My teeth are falling out.* Though they show no signs of looseness, no dark spots, no obvious cavities. He calls down a request for a dental consult. Forty-eight hours, they tell him. They're all away at a convention at Foxwoods.

Let her get hungry, Hyunjee says. She'll eat when she's hungry.

She isn't a three-year-old. Though, he might say, of course, on most days there isn't that much of a difference.

Well, what, then? IV nutrition?

Not now.

So what? We just let her stay like this?

That's what the expression means, he thinks: *suck the air out of a room*. They circle each other like wary lions; when she crosses the room to get a new bottle of moisturizer he moves around the far side of the bed, pretending, for the fifth time, to check the catheter bag. The room is stifling; she hasn't unbuttoned her sweater. At every opportunity she backs against a wall with her arms crossed. If he brushed her arm, let alone slid a palm against her waist, what would she do? Swat the offending appendage like a fly? He's tempted to find out. It's been four days, and he hasn't fully regained the use of his lower body; he still suffers from the occasional bolt of pure liquid joy.

The idea is to encourage them to make choices, he says. You know that. Choice is higher-level cognitive function.

It'll all go to waste.

You ought to make less, you know. You don't eat it.

She shoots him a nasty look. Fine. You try, then. See if she'll listen to you.

He pulls up a stool at the edge of the bed and pries open the lid of the smallest container. Kimchi. He can't eat it, though Hyunjee has offered many times: the smell makes his eyes water, but it's the image that gets him: the bulbous Napa roots, the rubbery leaves leaking bloody juices: like little hearts, scraps of human tissue, packed in a surgical basin.

Mama, he says loudly, and immediately, with no hesitation, she reaches out for the chopsticks, lifts a strand of cabbage out with great delicacy, and guides it to her mouth.

When we moved here, Hyunjee says, in '71, there wasn't a single other Korean family in Kew Gardens. Maybe fifty total in all of Queens. You couldn't buy a Napa cabbage in the whole borough, let alone the right kind of rice or *kochichang*. My aunt who lived in L.A. sent big boxes of supplies through the mail. When anyone flew back from Korea they would bring a suitcase full of sheets of nori. There was so little that after awhile she stopped forcing me to eat it. She cooked for her and Dad and let me boil hotdogs and eat mac and cheese. In public she let me speak back to her in English but at home she insisted on Korean. Thank god. I wanted out of the whole thing, right from the get-go. I was eleven, for Christ's sake.

Mrs. Kang digs out a hunk of rice and lifts it to her lips, her fingers trembling with the effort. As she chews her face takes on a puzzled, faraway look.

Seriously. Try to imagine it. You're a little girl, and someone pushes you down on the asphalt at recess, and you've got a skinned knee and your pants are torn, and you're crying and wishing your mother was there and not wishing your mother was there and wanting to speak Korean and not wanting to speak it. And nobody else knows what the difference is between you and Connie Choy in the seventh grade, nobody knows what a Korean *is*, or cares; aren't those places just all the same anyway? What matters is you're here. Nobody gives a shit about the Japanese invasion or President Rhee or the comfort women or two thousand years of this dynasty and that dynasty. You learn to hate your own inconvenient self.

And then before you know it you're in high school and you've forgotten all about it, you're just a good girl, a straight-A girl, you have your own little slot, and you ace the AP's and the only boys you talk to are the Jewish boys you debate in history class and kick the shit out of in calculus. And then one of them asks you to the prom, and you don't say no, you sneak out of the house through the basement window, and that's it, a quick sweaty fuck in the back of a rented limo. After that you're an American teenager for sure. Crying in the bathroom when your period's late.

She puts down the choptsticks, as if she's finished, then sticks our her fingers, picks another chunk of cabbage from the bowl, stares at it contemplatively, and tries to touch it to her lips; it winds around her finger, dribbing red juice down onto the knuckle.

All I'm saying is I'm sick of complications, Hyunjee says. I envy her sometimes. One language. One *place*. One set of memories. Sick, right? Sometimes I think human beings just weren't meant to live this way.

What way?

Oh, you know. So fucking *mixed up*. Spring rolls and matzoh balls. Filipinos doing your nails and Koreans doing your laundry and Guatemalans bringing your Chinese food and Hasids handing you pamphlets every time you come out of the subway. There comes a point where it has to stop, doesn't it? The human mind can't contain so many contradictions. I'm not trying to sound like a racist. It *isn't* racism to love your own kind. Whoever said we had to do penance for all historical sins by living in such an upside-down world? I'm tired of it.

Penance? he thinks. This is penance?

You know what the latest thing is? Samantha had this bright idea of having her bat mitzvah reception at one of the Korean barbeque places on 32nd Street. She *lives* for that stuff. And of course Stan's parents—well, they've been once, they know what it's like. Plates and plates of raw bloody meat. It's not that they're kosher, I'd hardly even call them observant. They might even agree to it. But they'd be humiliated, of course. *Devastated.* So I'm the one who has to drop that particular bomb on her. And of course she pulls out the whole routine: *I thought I could have anything I wanted. Am I supposed to, like, not be Korean, or something?* And all I want to say to her is, honey, you have no idea where this ends. *I* have no idea where it ends. And I'm tired of trying to explain it to them. You'd like to think they just accept it, because they don't know anything else. But they're not. They're climbing out of their bodies. It *isn't* natural. Like hell they'd ever be allowed to pray at the Wailing Wall.

I thought only men prayed there.

Oh, stop it. Don't quibble. You know what I mean.

She reaches out and holds her mother's chin still while he wipes the juice from her lips. Bright blossoms on each cheek, her ears flushed pink; lurid growths, poisonous mushrooms. Not for the first time he marvels at the vivid effects of pale skin, a taxonomy of stifled feeling. Is this what she means, he thinks, after so long, to still look at her as an instance, as a specimen?

I'm sorry, she says. I really should stop. I don't know what's taken hold of me. Maybe I'm coming down with something.

I'm a little dizzy. *Shit.* She gives him an anxious passing look; he can't help but notice the ripples of skin around her eyes, and how they never seem to move as much as they should, as much as he wants them to. *I've screwed everything up now, haven't I?*

He manages a dry chuckle, a little flourish of manly detachment. I know better than to think I know what to expect, he says.

But your situation is completely different. Wouldn't you say? You belong here. Your parents both spoke English, for Christ's sake. Irish and Jamaican—that's like the American dream. That makes sense.

Hyunjee, he says, be careful.

What does that mean?

When you're deciding what makes sense to *you.*

You want to know the worst thing about me? She gives him a wild-eyed, beseeching look, but it's purely formal, purely a warning: what is he supposed to do, run down the hall for a straitjacket, wrap her mouth shut with gauze tape? They put up that huge new mosque on 96th Street, she says, with the electric zipper sign on the fence, you know what I mean, and twenty-four hours a day it always says the same thing: *There is no God but Allah, and Mohammed is his prophet.* I pass it every time I drive out to Queens to go grocery shopping. And I always think, just for a second, I *hate* you. Every single time. I just want to stop the car and say, go back to fucking Egypt, if you're so sure. Go back to Saudi Arabia. Sometimes I'm just so sick of having to be polite. I'm just so sick of pretending that coexistence is easy or natural. It's like I'm allergic to New

York, but I am New York, after all; it's an auto-immune thing. Sometimes you have to think, No wonder someone wanted to drop a bomb on this place and start over. I mean, we're all sitting around, acting as if it's going to make sense someday, but it never, never will.

Well, he says, maybe you should go back to Korea and see what that's like. Leave the kids here. Leave them with what's-his-name. They'll do what kids always do. Survive. Adjust. *You* go back. If it means that much to you.

Her hands, beautiful, large, uncreased, unlined hands, don't know what to do with themselves; while she stares at him, her mouth puckering into a little triangular divot, as if halted in the midst of formulating a response, they move up and down her thighs, rubbing her pants pockets, as if she's not sure if she remembered her keys.

I don't get it, she finally says. Are you obtuse? You haven't been listening. Is that supposed to be funny?

Her face, once again: frozen in mid-look, eyebrows raised, as if surprised by any intensity, any feeling at all, even her own. Expecting to be hurt, he thinks, when he ought to be hurt; expecting it all to end badly.

All right, forget it. It was a rhetorical question.

You don't *rhetorically* tell someone to go back where they came from. I belong here. I paid my dues.

No one's suggesting otherwise.

And I'm not saying I'm a bad person, either. I appreciate what you did. It was a very sweet—no, a very—she waves a hand at the air, pinches the bridge of her nose, as if to let out the pressure of the thought. It was a gesture, he says. A somewhat disproportionate gesture. And I would love, believe me, I would love to respond in kind. But a life can only contain so much dissonance, don't you think? I'm just saying I'm *tired*.

No one ever suggested a relationship, he says, keeping his face blank. If that's what you mean. Did we misunderstand each other?

She shrugs and smooths the sheet around her mother's legs.

Because otherwise we would have to be very careful. Things could get awkward.

Is that a threat?

Of course not. It's an assessment. I'm not going anywhere until you say the word.

Well, then, she says, you don't have anything to worry about.

He's moved his bed to the far end of the room, away from the radiator, from the hot water pipes, underneath the window permanently propped open two inches with an old paperback copy of *The Fountainhead*. Never could sleep in heat of any kind. In the desert, when he was assigned the night shift and had to sleep in the glowing heat of the tent under the mid-day sun, he tore the liner out of his sleeping bag and soaked it with water out of his own precious supply. Like sleeping covered with wet paper towels. He's thought about moving his bed onto the roof, but not in Red Hook, not with six connected buildings on one block, and kids moving across them at all hours of the night with guns and yayo. On a good winter night the slipstream of cold air from the window keeps him happily underneath a pile of blankets. And so unable to hear the phone ringing on the most distant wall of the kitchen next to the stove. A railroad apartment, a run-to-the-phone apartment. His cell is turned off and charging on his bedside table.

It's too late to call, Hyunjee says. What time is it, anyway? Her voice is shaky, her breathing careless. I *knew* it was too late to call.

Hang up, he says. I'll see you tomorrow.

Oh, come on, she says. Don't sulk. I've been rehearsing this apology all night.

He lowers himself into a chair and props his bare feet on the table next to a dirty juice glass. In the sallow wash of the streetlights they look pale and knobby, angular. A starving man's feet. A runner's feet.

Listen, she says, those things I said, which I'm not going to repeat—

I remember them.

I was working something out. I was trying on a different frame of mind, and I'm sorry you had to be there to witness it. Sometimes I have to be the one person in the room who says what everybody else is thinking. Okay, okay, that's too presumptuous. What some people might be thinking. We're all so easily insulted these days, you know? Just quivering, waiting for someone to slip up so we can all take offense. It's just as tribal and parochial and dimwitted as the creationists in Kansas. Believe me, I should know. Offensive behavior is sending my kids to college.

Hyunjee, he says, you know what your problem is? You're too good at this game. You know you can talk your way out of anything.

So what, then? What's your solution? You were the one with all the questions the other night.

I'm just saying there are some problems talking can't solve.

Oh, she says. That old conundrum. Language is the sickness and the cure.

No, he's thinking, that's not how I would have put it. And then he has the impulse to say, to fire right back, love is the sickness and the cure. Shoot me now, he thinks, I've turned into a Hallmark card. And the worst of it is he's never believed any such thing. He would have said it without meaning it, to be clever, or provocative, to try it on for size. That's what you do around these people, he tells himself, you spatter words around like fingerpaint and call that a conversation, you say horrible things and take them back and say, that's a relationship, that's what I always wanted.

Hyunjee, he says, I accept your apology.

And just like that everything's back to normal?

No, he thinks, isn't that the point? Nothing was, nothing *is* ever normal. I'll see you tomorrow, he says, and lifts the heavy receiver away from his ear, holding her protesting voice between thumb and index fingers for a moment before dropping it, clattering, onto the cradle.

You make your own luck, his mother used to say, whenever someone waved around a lottery ticket or made a joke about four-leaf clovers. Easy come, easy go. I never had a stroke of it in my life and last I checked I'm okay. And then she would recite a speech by Michael Collins decrying the *national habits of passivity and despair.*

At Churchill's she drank Cokes with a slice of lemon, saying she'd promised her mother never to take anything stronger than communion wine.

Sorrowful men visited the house when he was young. Widowers, some of them, or men whose wives had run out. They were welcome at the table for two weeks and then came the scene in the living room. Some brought rings. or pictures of houses in Armonk or Jacksonville or Quogue. Frequently they wore their only suit and only tie. In his memory they are all fused into one, tall, gaunt, outrageous cheekbones, an Anthony Perkins type, whose elbows fly out like wings as he places his head in his hands. It seems like a melodramatic fifties movie; it seems like it can't have happened that way. His mother standing, hands on her hips. periodically reaching out to touch his shoulder. *Buck up*, she always seems to be saying, though surely she never said any such thing. *Don't you wish you could smother me. Don't you wish I needed you half as much.*

She was a force of nature, they said, one after another, at the funeral. After all, she was given to slapping Fathers and Monsignors on the back. She once wrote an impassioned letter to the *Catholic Reporter* arguing that divorced women ought to be allowed to take the habit. It was her only public concession that life may not have turned out exactly as planned.

Hoard your love, she said to him once. Don't waste it. Mark my words: it's not like water from the well. And, hearing the silent question, she turned, and laid a heavy hand across the doorjamb. Shame on you, she said. Shame on you for wondering. I've never been sorry.

She's popped an infection, the night nurse said on the phone. *Fever one-oh-two. They think it's the stent. Should I call her?* And he said, Ten minutes ago. Licking the dust of sleep off his lips. You know how she is. Get off and do it right now. Tell her I'm coming. *But it's four-thirty; don't I still get the rest of my shift?* Do it now! he shouts. Do it! And then clear out. Consider your ass fired.

Sorry, he keeps saying to Hyunjee, on the way back from the coffee machine, sorry, sorry. Should never have hired her. Should never have even looked at her twice.

Would you shut up?

Her skin, under the fluorescent lights, is shockingly grey. Corpselike. Raw-lipped, bare-eyed, in red Harvard sweat-pants and a hooded sweater. She backs into the wall of the elevator and closes her eyes.

I mean, it looks like they've got it under control, right? The drug's working. I shouldn't bring the girls in to say goodbye, right?

She'll still be here in the morning.

Then go home. I'll stay.

Is that really what you want?

I don't think you should work for me any longer, she says, opening her eyes and staring past him at the wall. I mean, I'll pay you. I'll keep paying you. What, a month's severance, two months, is that fair?

He laughs, the dazed, punch-drunk laugh all nurses have, at the end of the graveyard shift. He can't help himself. Hyunjee, he says, you think that'll make it better? A golden handshake?

I made a mistake, okay? Distractedly she undoes the haphazard knot holding her hair in place, and lets it fall across her forehead, the streak of grey curving like a nautilus shell. I needed someone to be objective, she says, flicking the hair back with her thumb. Not that I thought I wasn't a good daughter. Not that I felt guilty. But she deserves more than that, you know? Everybody deserves more than one. It wasn't her fault that they didn't know what endometriosis *was* back in those days. It's not that she wanted a son. She just wanted a second try. And she was right, goddamn it! Nobody should ever be so fucking alone that they have to hire strangers to be family. I'm sorry. I can't help myself. Here, hold this.

She holds out her coffee cup to him, and zips her sweater up to the neck, and begins to cry, dropping her hands in front of her like a rag doll, and when he embraces her, when he covers her face with his chest, does not raise them, does not wrap them around his waist, but shrinks into him, into herself, like a dried-out stem, he thinks, like a twig, clasping his awkward paws around her with a styrofoam cup of hot liquid in each, like urine samples, or blood vials, anything vital, anything carrying the body's warmth away.

This is the way to tell the story. When the grandchildren ask, how was it that they met, those two, a Portuguese sailor and an ex-nun from Estonia, or, how did they communicate, if he didn't speak Finnish and she didn't speak Taiwanese. You don't say, He was already drunk when they met in the airport bar. Or, they were locked in the basement accidentally for three hours before the manager let them out. You say, in this case there was no other way. The world is made choice after choice after choice in the singular present tense. The body makes logic; not the other way around.

And then they ask, is it fair, is it just, to reduce it to that? To subject us to your whims? Is it the height of selfishness, these willy-nilly associations, this refusal to plan, this projecting the future from the momentary bubble of your own ego?

Well, you say, which is it better to be seduced by: the future in the form of a woman with hair the color of streaming silver, with hands like water, or the future in the form of an organizing principle?

Samantha, she says, when he backs open the door in the morning, his arms full of new bedding. Samantha. Pearl. Turn around. I want you to say hi to Kevin.

They turn away from the bed awkwardly, darting looks at one another: *It's just the nurse. It's just the nurse, right?* Hi, the older one says, flipping her bangs back. Tiny bright green eyes. Um, thanks for taking such good care of grandma.

I'm Pearl, the little one says. Yeah, thanks.

Kevin's coming out to lunch with us. Aren't you?

There's no one to take over. I'd have to make a call.

It's all right. Just an hour.

Aren't you kids supposed to be in school?

In-service. Pearl sucks a lollipop, knocking it against her teeth. Professional development day.

Something is sticking in his throat, a crooked knuckle, a little jagged stone. He can't look at them straight on. Little suns, he thinks, little flames of the future. Their shifting brown limbs, their twitching fingers. Outrageous, the claims they make on us! Outrageous, the way they judge us from thirty years hence!

So, Hyunjee asks, interrupting his reverie. Are you coming or not?

It makes a kind of tableau, he thinks, a frieze, these women's faces, women and soon-to-be women, waiting to see what he'll do next. As if in some obscure way that's what he's always wanted. *The measure of a man.* Behind the girls, Mrs. Kang stirs, wraps her blue fingers around the rail, and pulls her face a few inches up from the pillow.

I never had a son, she says. *Nahantaen adeul op da!* I don't know who you are.

The Answer

Say it's a Thursday afternoon in late August. Say that much to begin with. I'm sitting in the grass on Old Campus with my roommates, waiting for First Year Orientation to begin. A cloudless day, painfully bright, smelling of mowed lawns and sweat: the sun burning the backs of our necks like an angry eye.

In the middle of one of those strange conversations freshmen have when they first meet—breathless confessions, punctuated by abrupt, uncomfortable silences—I cast about for somewhere else to look, and see a tall Hispanic boy standing a little distance from us, his arms folded, scowling at Connecticut Hall through thick square glasses.

I'm not a gregarious person by nature. I've never been aggressively social. But it's the first week of freshman year, and already I'm a little lonely, sensing that Michael and Jake will stop speaking to one another, and me, in a month. Hey, man, I say, leaning toward him on one elbow, trying to look relaxed. Are you in Trumbull? What's your name?

He sits with great delicacy, as if he doesn't have much experience lowering himself to the ground. Despite the heat he has on a pair of stiff new jeans, rolled up at the ankles, and an untucked, long-sleeved dress shirt. Dark patches of sweat stand out against his collarbones. Rafael, he says, once he's arranged himself with legs folded. His voice nearly drowned out by the faint music blaring from a window on the other side of the quadrangle. I'm from Delaware, he says. Wilmington, Delaware.

No shit? I'm from Baltimore. Just down the road from you.

He doesn't smile, or nod, or change his expression at all: his mouth hangs slightly open, waiting to see what I will do next. In the corner of my eye Michael and Jake give one another significant looks.

So what room are you in?

He turns and points to the window just above mine.

Two-thirteen. But there is a problem. I have to change.

What's wrong with it?

We have only one bathroom.

There's something strange about his way of speaking: he hesitates an instant too long after each phrase, with a faint smile, as if mentally translating word-by-word. Not a Spanish accent: it seems, oddly, Eastern European, or Russian. As if to say, like an old émigré, *English isn't really adequate, but what can you do?*

There are girls across the hall, he says. I have to share with them.

So what? So do we. So does everyone. It's Yale policy.

He folds his hands in his lap and stares down at the grass between us. I'm a Muslim, he says. It's not proper.

Jake bites his lip, *chews* his lip, trying not to laugh.

Well, there must be something they can do, I tell him. They can find you a different room somewhere. Did you tell them that when you sent in your roommate forms?

His eyelids dip slowly, and he fixes me with a sour look, an old man's tired frown. Yes, he says, impatiently.

Shouldn't that be the end of the story? *I'm here,* his face says. *Isn't that enough for you? Do I have to explain myself again, every step of the way?* Across the lawn a whistle shrieks, and eight hundred of us stand all at once, trying not to appear too eager, tugging out the legs of our sweaty shorts. Rafael stays seated, and I next to him, in a half-crouch, a helper's pose.

(I'm not blind to subtext. Say, for argument's sake, that my heart is temporarily opened. Say that a look of torment fixes me to the ground.)

And then he stands up and dusts himself off and twists away.

The year—I should mention this, shouldn't I? The year is 1993.

We spend the next few days shuttling from one meeting and training session to another. We learn to recognize the signs of eating disorders and the signs of depression; to avoid sexual assault by travelling in groups; to understand that no means no; to squeeze the tip of the condom before you roll it on; to avoid muggings by traveling in groups; to give homeless people vouchers for food instead of money; to speak to our R.A.'s if we feel angry, hurt, lost, anorexic, depressed, or sexually assaulted; to avoid unpleasant encounters with roving townies by traveling in groups. Rafael isn't anywhere to be seen, and his name never comes up in any conversation, not even the ones you might expect: This guy, across the hall? You wouldn't believe it, he's some kind of super-orthodox *Muslim*?

A week later, when I see him staring into a plate of green beans and baked fish in the Trumbull dining hall, I've forgotten him altogether. He raises his head just as I'm scanning the tables, looking for a familiar face, and our eyes meet. By accident. He's sitting alone, and instantly I know—we both know—it would be unforgivably rude for me not to join him, though I'm in a hurry, and the last thing I want is to get involved.

I know you, he says, when I introduce myself again. We met the first day. On the grass. He doesn't smile, but gives me a tiny nod, a slight inclining of the head. Isaac is a very interesting name, he says. Not everyone would choose that name.

Yeah. A little too Biblical. I went through a stage of trying to get people to call me Zack, but there were two other Zacks in my class at school. And the funny thing is that my town is mostly Jewish, and my high school was mostly Jewish, and *I'm* the one named Isaac.

He cuts a chunk of scrod with his fork and lifts it up, picking away the bones carefully. I assume you know the story of Ibrahim and the sacrifice, he says. The Jewish-Christian version. He unfolds his napkin carefully, as if it were an old document, a tattered map from the glove box, and uses one corner of it to wipe his mouth. But you haven't heard the Muslim version. Ibrahim has two sons, right? Isaac and Ismail. So God—Allah—asks him to make this sacrifice, and when Ibrahim refuses, Allah says, this son, who you were willing to sacrifice, he will be the father of the chosen people.

And the sons of Ishmael are the outcasts.

Right. A broad smile. Only, you know, in our way of looking at things, Ismail is the chosen one, and Isaac is the outcast.

Well, I say, it's just two sides of the same coin, isn't it? It's not as if Isaac did anything special. God could just as well have blessed them both. It could be all an argument over translation. Isaac or Ishmael—what if the scribes got it wrong?

Don't be ridiculous. The text is crystal-clear.

I don't think anything in the Bible is crystal-clear.

Let me guess, he says, expressionless, spearing beans with his fork. Your parents must be Episcopalians.

Unitarians. Does that make a difference?

As if satisfied, in some obscure way, he looks up at the rafters of the dining hall, at the shields with heraldric crests and Latin mottos underneath the leaded-glass windows, and nods, distractedly. Go ahead, I want to say to him, insult me. Get it over with. I've already picked my way through my own plate of overcooked fettucine and too-sweet tomato sauce; and it's time for me to consider the other options: the salad bar, the bagel bar, another peanut-butter-and-jelly sandwich, a merciful quick escape to the library. An unfamiliar taste rises in my throat, like bile: the sour-bitter sting of a swallowed argument.

You want to know what I think? he asks, his eyes widening, as if he's just remembered where he is. The winners have all the options. They can choose to feel about themselves however they want. They can even choose not to be winners anymore. Isn't that amazing? Never underestimate the power of guilt. That shit makes the world go round.

I wouldn't know, I say, staring straight at him. I don't know anything about guilt.

Is that so, he says, sucking his teeth. Then I guess you must be the only one.

Isn't it a little too implausible that I would hear a knock at my door two days later, at an hour when Jake and Michael happen to be out, and find Rafael standing there? Or that I would invite him in? I myself find it hard to believe. Can the world have ever been quite so cinematically innocent, so porous, so unparanoid?

Bear with me. For the purposes of this story, believe that it was.

He looks helpless and bewildered, clutching a textbook and a ragged notebook under his arm, wearing the same jeans as before and a white t-shirt that hangs halfway down his thighs. The outfit reminds me, uncomfortably, of a movie I've seen about Chicano gangsters in prison. Stop it, I tell myself, with a little quiver of disgust, an instinctual tightening of my stomach muscles, my sphincter. As I could expel the image by a sheer act of will.

I'm sorry to bother you, he says, formally, as if he's been standing in front of my door practicing what to say. Are you studying for the psychology test tomorrow? I'm having a hard time with it. Can I come in?

In our common room—a futon, a halogen lamp, a stack of milk crates for bookshelves, a Dinosaur Jr. poster, a Rothko print, a stereo perched precariously on the box it came in—he looks awkwardly from side to side, almost twitching with discomfort. Finally I point him to the futon and move my desk chair to face him.

It's this influence stuff, he says, opening the textbook across his knees. This part. *The human mind has an overwhelming craving for stability and symmetry, particularly in social relationships with strangers. Schloss (1967) demonstrated that adult subjects who feel an obligation imposed on them (even one they did not choose themselves) will make every effort to fulfill it, and report feeling unsettled and anxious if prevented from doing so. The same logic applies to all free-giveaway programs and one-on-one selling techniques.*

That's easy. Without meaning to I've taken on a professor's stance, one elbow propposed precariously on the bookshelf. Think of the example he gave in lecture. The Hare Krishna guy comes up to you in the airport and gives you a sticker that says "Smile!" without asking you for permission first. Even if you don't want the sticker, he won't take it back, and you can't throw it away in front of him—that would be rude. So you have to talk to him for thirty seconds. That gives him time to make the pitch for his children's charity, or whatever he's trying to collect money for. Again, because he initiated the relationship with a gift, you still feel indebted, so you might wind up giving him a dollar or two or five, Even though you know better.

He takes off his glasses and wipes them on the hem of his t-shirt. It's a warm night, still now in mid-September, and the creases in his forehead are shiny with sweat. Without his glasses, slightly flushed by the heat, he looks naked, defenseless as a newborn. Except, I notice now, he has a small white scar at the left corner of his mouth, a cut badly healed.

Only an idiot would act that way, he says. Doesn't it just seem like nonsense to you? All this manipulation, all these tricks?

They're assuming everybody has the same unconscious. And why should that be? Think about it. Why should some professor know what *my* unconscious is like?

The studies are all supposed to be multi-ethnic. They factor that part in.

He laughs, the one and only time I will ever hear him laugh, a deep guffaw out of the belly that is also like a suppressed groan. Bullshit they do, he says, all these studies are done on college campuses, so who do you expect they're going to find?

Then why take psychology? I ask him. If you've already decided you don't believe in it, why take it?

Leaning back, he tilts his head up to stare at the ceiling, and lets his hands fall uselessly on the textbook's open page, fingers curling skyward. The futon creaks underneath him. Everyone has to learn a skill, he says, tonelessly, as if repeating a line learned in childhood. The Movement doesn't need illiterates. It needs doctors, lawyers, engineers. People with degrees. The new nation depends on those people.

Without looking at me, he digs into the pocket of his jeans and thrusts a battered yellow pamphlet in my direction.

Jihaad In The Cause of God
Young Muslims United, Toronto, CANADA
for free distribution.

The paper tissue-thin, the type a reprint of an older edition, printed on an inferior press, hardly legible in places. In my hands it falls open to a paragraph highlighted in orange.

This religion is really a universal declaration of the freedom of man from servitude to other men and from servitude to his own desires, which is also a form of human servitude; it is a declaration that sovereignty belongs to God alone and that He is the Lord of all the worlds. It means a challenge to all kinds and forms of systems which are based on the concept of the sovereignty of man; in other words, where man has usurped the Divine attribute. This declaration means that the usurped authority of God be returned to Him and the usurpers be thrown out. In short, to proclaim the authority and sovereignty of God means to eliminate all human kingship and to announce the rule of the Sustainer of the universe over the entire earth.

I turn a few pages and start again.

As we have described earlier, there are many practical obstacles in establishing God's rule on earth, such as the power of the state, the social system and traditions and, in general, the whole human environment. Islam uses force only to remove these obstacles so that there may not remain any wall between Islam and individual human beings, and so that it may address their hearts and minds after releasing them from these material obstacles, and then leave them free to choose to accept or reject it.

What does this part mean? *There are many obstacles in establishing God's rule on earth, such as the whole human environment?*

He lifts his head and looks at me curiously.

Why? What do you *think* it is?

Well, what else is there? *God's* environment?

Exactly.

That's a circular argument. If you define God as everything

not human and yet say that we're supposed to destroy our own environment and accept God's—

Shut up and listen for a second. Tiny drops of sweat trickle down his forehead, and he wipes them away with the back of his hand. This isn't just philosophy, he says. It's a *program*. The first people going down are the governments of Egypt, Jordan, and Saudi Arabia. It's all about reclaiming the Islamic world and making it real. Not just a copy of the West. Those countries have their laws, and we have *shari'a*. We don't want to force anybody to become Muslims, but we want Muslims to be allowed to *be* Muslims.

As he speaks he squares his shoulders and leans forward, elbows on his knees, watching me, watching the room. Projecting. Did he learn that in theater class, I'm wondering, and if so, can he tell I have a trick of my own, pressing my tongue against the roof of my mouth to keep from smiling?

I know what you're thinking. He flicks his fingers dismissively. Yeah, I was a Catholic. I went to Catholic school through eighth grade. Does that make you happy? You want to hear about how my mother waded across the Rio Grande with only her shoes in a plastic bag?

Look, I say, you have to admit it's a little incongruous. Who's to say you won't decide to give it up in another year?

And who's to say you won't be a Muslim yourself in another year?

He stands and walks over to my desk, arms crossed, peering at the CDs piled along the windowsill, reading the posters and postcards I've taped to the wall above.

Cat Stevens is a Muslim. You like Cat Stevens, don't you?

I turn around in my chair to face him, as he bends over my desk, scanning the papers and open books curiously, dispassionately, as if looking at a museum display under glass.

Is that how you recruit new members? *Cat Stevens?*

He closes his eyes.

Islam has nothing to do with violence, he says. If you try it—if you pray, if you read the Quran, if you come to the *masjid,* you'll understand. And I really think you should, Isaac. Because I can tell that you're not happy. You may think you belong here, but you don't. Not really. No more than I do.

I have a curious tickling feeling at the back of my throat, as if I've swallowed something dry and scratchy by accident; I cough, once, twice, but it doesn't change.

What makes you so sure of that?

His smile lifts up only one corner of his mouth, at once wistful and patronizing. Why else would you be sitting here talking to me for so long? he says. Shouldn't you have somewhere else to be? He picks up his textbook and the pamphlet, tucks them under his arm, and pauses for a moment, his head lifted, reading another poster I've tacked to my closet door. A sepia-toned picture of Rilke, and a quotation from *Letters to a Young Poet:*

> *The point is to live everything. Live the questions now. Perhaps then, someday far in the future, you will gradually, without even noticing it, live your way into the answer.*

Have you read Rilke? I'll lend you his books if you want.

He shakes his head in a kind of spasm, as if coming out of a momentary trance.

It's not so hard, he says, giving me a sly, sideways smile. Why should you have to wait so long?

The next day is a Thursday, and I wake up late, having missed my nine o'clock English class, with a headache and a mouth that feels stuffed with cotton batting. The sky is the color of wet cement and the air has a faint metallic chill, a fall feeling, for the first time. All day, following familiar paths across campus, I have a slight sense of drift, of not quite following a straight path from point A to point B. The cries of the woman who stands at the corner of York and Elm—*a flower for a dollar! Please, sir, a flower for a dollar!*—follow me down the block. In my philosophy class, describing Socrates' final words in the *Phaedo,* the professor, who walks with a limp and seems nearly eighty, turns his face to the blackboard for a full minute, as if looking over his shoulder at someone, and then returns to his lecture with no explanation.

That night, at dinner, I strike up a conversation with two guys I've never met before, sophomores, and afterwards we go up to their room to listen to a live Coltrane date from 1966, and smoke pot, three bowls, until the lights in the room take on a bluish tinge and the music thickens into a single vibrating pulse. After midnight, walking back alone across Old Campus, I see a light still on in a second-floor window, just above mine: Rafael's window.

Sovereignty is God's alone, and he is the ruler of all the worlds.

Without having quite meant to, I've veered off the stone walkway and come to a halt on the grass. A faint breeze ruffles the leaves of an oak tree off to the right. No one else is around;

a long uninterrupted row of discs of light stretches underneath the security lamps, like a line of white coins. Inside these buildings one thousand-odd seventeen- and eighteen-year-olds, sleeping, smoking, fucking, leaning out of windows, mastering Russian grammar and particle physics, writing first novels, playing erotic games of Scrabble, but how many of them *know*, and know they know, the truth?

Is truth what we're paying for?

Sovereignty is God's alone, and he is the ruler of all the worlds.

He doesn't look surprised when he opens the door.

Come in, he says. His accent thicker than the day before. I was just cleaning up. Have a seat.

The room has no furniture to speak of. A mattress in one corner, a plastic milk crate upended for a desk, a line of books against the wall, white t-shirts and dark jeans piled on top of a suitcase. Even the glass ceiling lamp has been removed, and the bare bulb gives off a yellowish glare. On the wall above the bed a calendar with a picture of a sunrise and Arabic writing across it. He's not staying long, I tell myself, immediately, involuntarily. This is an encampment.

I talked to one of the maintenance guys, he says. I told him if he took away everything he could sell it if he wanted to.

I sit down on the edge of the mattress, clasping my knees together. My mouth has gone dry, and the harsh light makes my eyes ache. I've forgotten whatever it was I planned to say.

It's cool. You've got a lot more space this way. It's very monastic.

All that shit is unnecessary, he says. It glorifies the body. Allah wants us to make palaces in his name and live in tents outside them. On tiptoe, he stretches out his arm and almost touches the ceiling. All this construction, he says, all this money. I mean, okay, it's a cold climate, you can't live outside all the time, the way they do in Arabia. But they could have had some humility, you know what I mean? This is a student dormitory, not a fucking castle. You went on the tour, didn't you? All these buildings were put up in the 1930's, but they wanted to make them look old. So they poured acid on the roof tiles and broke the glass in the windows so it'd look all funky and crooked. Man, if that's not a symbol of a civilization in decline, I don't know what is. A bunch of pathetic white geezers who have all this money and so little to show for it that they have to make an imitation of something that's six hundred years old.

He bends his knees and jumps in place, landing on his heels with a bang, as if to test the strength of the floor.

You want to know the truth? he asks. America is the most self-hating society the world has ever seen. Why else would all these rich folks decide that they're going to take the people they've chained, whipped, shat upon, and murdered for the last four hundred years, select the best ones, and give them all the tools they need to take over? Sure, they get a few lapdogs here and there. Colin Powell, Clarence Thomas. Bill Cosby. But over time they're signing their own death warrant, and they know it. If those people really knew how to run a society they would have listened to Henry Ford back in the thirties.

Henry Ford?

He was Hitler's biggest fan. Didn't you study any of this

shit? He was the only one of them who was willing to tell the truth. A society based on money is a society based on murder. That's rule number one. Money creates envy on one side and fear on the other. And where does the urge to murder come from? Envy or fear. It's just that basic. Hatred is the gas in the engine. The problem is, how do you use it? That's what Hitler understood. People like us, we need to kill. We have to hate somebody. It's in our blood. You can sublimate it, you can ignore it, you can hand out scholarships and welfare and what-all, but that only lasts so long. Hatred is power. It has to be channeled.

The sticky haze of the pot is beginning to clear; every time I blink I can see the room more clearly, its bright surfaces and hard-edged shadows. It isn't that I've never heard these things before. Baltimore has its share of street-corner prophets; vendors of *The Spartacist* and *Revolutionary Worker* and *The Final Call*. All the rusting Eastern cities do. If you're a curious fifteen-year-old out walking the streets for the first time, playing at independence, little more than bus fare in your pockets, you stop and listen to them. You take the pamphlet extolling the virtures of the Shining Path and the FMLN button and sign the petitions to free political prisoners you've never heard of. And you never, ever respond, because they don't want questions; because it's a performance, not a dialogue. They have bright tubercular eyes, they are incapable of embarrassment, and they never tire.

But you can't do it, I'm thinking. You can't be a shoeless prophet in the Berkeley College Dining Hall, underneath the chandeliers and the mounted ibex. It's there in invisible ink, in all the pages you sign. You take on that mantle of shame. The gate you don't see is the gate that closes behind you. It's the smell of the steam vents, the boiled food, the carving of Confucius over the library door. When you come to Yale you relinquish the right to be a mad prophet and scrabble around in the entrails of birds. You refuse to call the president a blue-eyed devil, until you can prove it in a chemical equation, or refer to it, in passing, in a devastating parenthetical. You take on the humiliation of belonging.

Adult subjects who feel an obligation imposed on them (even one they did not choose themselves) will make every effort to fulfill it, and report feeling unsettled and anxious if prevented from doing so. The same logic applies to all free-giveaway programs and one-on-one selling techniques.

With the kind of confidence only a college freshman can have, I look up, I hold his gaze, his unblinking eyes, rimmed with baby fat, and say, in a hoarse whisper, Rafael, give it up. You know I don't hate you.

He squats in front of me, angling his face to one side, so that I see it in profile. See this scar? he asks, pointing. You know how I got it? A rat bit me while I was sleeping. When I was three. We were in some welfare hotel in South Carolina, and they evicted us, and it was raining, so we slept in the back, in the shed where they kept the dumpsters. When my mom took me to the hospital they refused to give me rabies shots because she couldn't provide any ID. If that isn't hate, then what is? Those people *wanted* me dead.

But—

And you can say that it's not fair, he says, you can say that I can't extrapolate, you know, that I can't tar you with the same brush, or whatever. But here's the truth. I do. *We* do. We're hard-wired to. And don't give me this nature-or-nurture, humanistic, free-will asinine liberal bullshit about *individual worth and dignity*. That's the biggest lie of all. As if anything in this world was really about individuals.

Hold on. I stick a finger out at him, as if to say, *enough*, as if it's not much too late for *enough*. I respect your right to say, *based on my experience, I believe*—almost anything. But you can't tell me that *I* hate *you*. Step back for a minute. The world is more complicated than that.

He turns partway toward me and grips the back of his neck with both hands, covering his ears with his wrists. You don't get it at all, he says, closing his eyes. Not that I'd really expect you to. But it's sad. It's really fucking sad. Because the point of all of this, the reason for my saying this, is that the only solution is total submission to God. Once you admit to yourself that you've spent your life worshipping false idols, and your heart is full of confusion and darkness and buried rage and guilt and lust, only then can you allow Allah into your heart. I'm talking about peace and serenity like nothing you've ever known. And you, Isaac, I thought you would understand this. Everybody can see it in your face, man. You're lost. You don't know what to believe. You're a wide-open door. You've got all this power and privilege, but that's not enough. You're sick of this dream country.

Outside, in the entryway, shuffling steps on the stairs, and a loud girl's voice. I can't believe you've never had Jell-O shots before, she's saying. You have to take it slow. They put a ton of vodka in them, didn't you know that? Watch it! Hold the rail.

I don't have any power, I want to tell him. *I'm not special. Why did you have to choose me? Who do you think I am?*

And what if you're right? What then?

I've still got my scholarship checks. He starts to sway back and forth, ducking, bobbing his head, and then begins to dance like a boxer, on the balls of his feet, whipping his arms out in careless punches. The bursar's office is after me. They've been banging on my door every day since I got here. If I go now I'll still have enough for a one-way ticket to Karachi. He spins, hammering at the air; he throws a roundhouse kick over my head. I met this guy in Jersey City who gave me the number of his mosque. He said they're always looking for Americans. You can go to school there for free; they'll teach you Arabic, the Koran, everything you need to know. It's all paid for by charity. That's the thing, man. It's a system. It's a new way to live. They're taking lost people from everywhere, people like us, and giving them a new life. All you have to do is show up.

He pulls up the hem of his t-shirt and wipes his face with it. Underneath his torso is the color of putty. As if he never takes his shirt off, as if he's never been outside barechested, not once, not in a swimming pool or on a beach.

You can get the money, he says. The ticket's about fifteen hundred. Your parents probably gave you that much to start your bank account, didn't they?

Rafael, I say, smiling, shaking my head. Don't be an idiot.

Why not? he asks. Am I wrong? I haven't heard you arguing. Do you disagree with my analysis? Then tell me what *you* think. Don't just fucking sit there.

I respect your opinion. That's as far as I'll go. I'm willing to give you the benefit of the doubt.

Oh, Jesus, he says, what a classic liberal evasion, man, that's the way to defuse any argument, isn't it? They teach you that shit in the womb, don't they? *Let's agree to disagree. Fuck* that! he says, slapping his palm against the wall. Come on, articulate something, why don't you? Why shouldn't I go to Pakistan? Now's your chance, Isaac. You've got thirty seconds.

He stares at me with such intensity that I have to look away; a biological reaction, probably, going back to our days in the trees. All animals know that eye contact is hostile, that meeting an angry gaze is open warfare. I have to force myself to look up again, to see him. And when I do, of course, I know how afraid he is. His forehead creases; his eyelids perform little spasms, narrowing and widening, as if he's waiting for me to jump up and attack.

I can't tell you anything new. You've worked it out to your own satisfaction. It's useless for me to say that *I* don't believe that Henry Ford was right. You know that already. And you know that I'm not going with you, either. You're afraid of leaving without somebody knowing why.

You're underestimating me.

The problem, I say, ignoring him, is that I don't think you really believe in this stuff. You've talked yourself into a corner and you can't get out, but that's not the same thing as a conversion. Islam is all about God's love, right? You don't *have* any fucking love. You need a shrink, not a new religion. So I'm not going to be your witness, all right? You can't put me in that position. Go do what you want, but don't ask me to legitimize it. As far as you're concerned, I was never here. I never listened to this.

He gives me a knowing grin, his lips pulled back against the teeth. You can be cruel, he says. But I guess I should have expected that. That's the badge of the do-gooder class, ain't it? *My way or the highway.*

You asked for my opinion.

I asked for an argument, not a psychiatric evaluation. He opens the door a few inches. You can go now, he says. That's what you want, right?

I stand up, unsteadily; my legs have gone to sleep, and I have to bend over and massage them before I can walk. As I approach the door, he doesn't move; he stands with his arms at his sides, like a sentry, half-blocking my way, so that I'll have to push past him to get by.

When you get sick of this place, he says, when you realize I'm right, come join me. I'll still be there. I'm not coming back.

I believe you.

Don't believe me. Believe God.

He lunges forward, takes my right hand, presses the palm against his face. He hasn't shaved; he doesn't shave. Soft skin, oily, rubbery. Human skin. I haven't been touched in nearly a month. Not a hug, not a caress, not an arm over my shoulder. College students don't shake hands.

This body is just a shell, he says, it's a tool in God's hands, for him to use and throw away. Don't listen to my voice. Trust God speaking through me. Look at the movie, not the screen. *This is the life you want.* This is the call. It won't come again.

I pull my hand away; I move into the gap between his shoulder and the doorjamb, and he turns with me, one body to another, like a dancer, and presses his mouth for a moment against mine. And what is it, what can I call it, inertia, or terror, or are they one and the same, keeps me moving, unclasping from his embrace like a hand releasing from a handshake. If I could speak I would say, *it's not enough. I wish it was. It's not enough.* At the bottom of the stairs, wiping my mouth, I hear his door slam.

Appendix 1

In ten years I only thought about Rafael Mendes once.

It was at a party in Cambridge, in the summer, on someone's back porch. We were sitting in a semicircle of chairs drinking sangria—a few friends from graduate school, wives, boyfriends, neighbors. The woman next to me was named Erin; she lived up the street, and, as it turned out, she was a forensic pathologist at Brigham and Women's, a researcher who specialized in scars, wounds, abscesses—the icky stuff, she said. She had slender white legs and little explosions of red freckles all over her face and shoulders, and she wasn't above sticking her fingers into her glass to retrieve the grapes.

I had a friend in college with a scar on his face from a rat bite, I told her.

I'm not sure why. I said it lightly, casually, as a bit of polite conversation; I hardly even remembered who it was I was referring to. Don't we all do that, sometimes, just for the sake of having something to say? I described it, how it stood out against the skin, and used my pinky to indicate the size.

She frowned and shook her head.

I hate to tell you this, she said, but your friend was making that up. Rat bites aren't that big, to begin with. And they gouge, they don't slice. To me that sounds more like a knife wound. Probably he cut himself playing when he was a kid. She bit into a chunk of apple. Points for creativity, though, she said. A *rat bite*? Only kids in the projects get those. He wasn't Puerto Rican, was he?

He might have been. I never asked.

Well, she said, I grew up in New York, and the Puerto Rican kids at my school always used to say that if you ratted out your friends to the teachers or the cops you'd get cut like that on the side of your mouth. They called it the *chismo*. Or sometimes *la rata*. Maybe he was being poetic. It's not the kind of thing you'd want to admit, is it? Even years later. You should look him up and see what he says now.

She crossed her legs and smoothed the front of her sundress, a little nervously, as if afraid she'd said too much. Like so many women my age, I thought, apologizing for her expertise, hesitating to be an authority.

And you, she said, what do you do? You haven't said a word about yourself.

It's all right, I said. My friend, the one I was talking about? He used to say that individuals don't really matter.

Her lips formed a vague smile, a place holder, while she looked around the room for an explanation. What is it with you people, she asked, finally. Why do you insist on telling jokes no one else gets?

Appendix 2

From the *Washington Post*, October 7, 2003:

American Jihadist Reported Killed In Cairo Bombing

Rafael Mendes, a 28-year-old Delaware resident reported missing ten years ago, was reported to have been killed Friday in a failed suicide bombing near the British embassy in Cairo, according to news reports in the Egyptian press over the weekend.

Mendes, who disappeared shortly after enrolling at Yale University as a freshman in 1993, apparently had spent time in Pakistan and Afghanistan, and at some point changed his name to Mustafa Ali, according to a report in Al-Ahram Newsweekly, which quoted an anonymous member of the radical group he was associated with.

Mendes appears to have been the sole occupant of a truck filled with explosives which exploded after striking a low overpass about a mile from the British embassy. The overpass collapsed in the explosion, killing a bicycle rider and injuring twenty motorists.

His parents, Marco and Rosa Mendes, of Wilmington, were notified of the reports by the State Department yesterday. In an interview with a local television crew, Mr. Mendes said they had heard from Rafael only once, in 1995, in a postcard sent from Islamabad, in which he wished them well and advised them to build a bomb shelter underneath their house in order to "avoid the coming Holocaust."

Mr. Mendes, who owns a trucking company, said that Rafael had a "normal" childhood and was an exceptionally bright student who won a full scholarship to Yale.

"He was every parent's dream," Mr. Mendes said. "He never got into

any trouble. All this stuff about Islam just came out of nowhere the summer before he left for Yale. We figured it was just a phase, and he'd grow out of it once he got to college. The next thing we knew he disappeared."

Appendix 3

From Walter Benjamin, "Theses on the Philosophy of History":

To articulate the past does not mean to recognize it "the way it really was." It means to seize hold of a memory as it flashes up at a moment of danger.

Appendix 4

It's the first week in November.

I'm sitting crosslegged, alone, on a bench on the Green, reading the *Oresteia*. Having gone there to avoid my roommates' furious glances across the common room. It's too cold to be sitting outside, but I'm stubborn; I've pulled the sleeves of my jacket down over my hands, leaving only the knuckles exposed. On the opposite side of the path, about twenty feet away, a homeless man or woman is asleep under a pile of newspapers and dirty clothes, his head—or hers—hidden under a torn piece of blue carpet.

> *For we are strong and skilled;*
> *we have authority; we hold*
> *memory of evil; we are stern*
> *nor can men's pleadings bend us. We*

drive through our duties, spurned, outcast
from gods, driven apart to stand in light
not of the sun.

I look up just as the pale autumn sun dips behind the Taft, and all at once I am gripped by a heart-wringing sadness. The three churches on the Green stand deserted, like decorations, placed there as an afterthought. Most of the storefronts along Chapel Street are empty and dark. The cold is soaking into my bones. I ought to go over to the figure lying on the ground and shake him, and say, *it's too cold to stay out, you need to get to a shelter,* but you don't do that here; too many of them are paranoid, or drunk, or high, and you could get stabbed, or worse. Human beings freeze to death in this city from time to time. You learn to live with it, and with the police sirens racing past your window every night, and the faint pops in the distance that might or might not be gunshots.

Rafael, I think, this broken world will never be mended.

My face is turning numb. I stand up, stiffly, and shake out my arms, trying to get the blood flowing. I'm witnessing something; I know that much. Say that for a moment it's possible to cut the fabric of our days and expose the fulcrum, the glistening gears, the smell of grease. I ought to lie down on the ground myself. I should hail a cab for the airport and buy a ticket to Karachi and find a way to bring him back.

If I could find a way to walk out of this story, I would. Instead, I turn and walk back toward Phelps Gate, toward the dark battlements lying in shadow, because I have nowhere else to go.

Sheep May Safely Graze

It was a tiny leak, no more than a pinprick, and a few eyedroppers full of gas that killed my youngest daughter, Jolie, at summer camp when she was eight years old. She was in a motorboat on Lake St. Clair, learning to waterski. The fuel line ruptured; gas leaked into the bilge, and when the driver started the engine the boat exploded. The two other girls next to her on the rear seat, in lifejackets, also died. The driver, who should have checked the fuel tanks, who should have smelled the gas—a nineteen-year-old, named Rick Paradisi—suffered third-degree burns over most of his body and survived for three months in a coma.

The story was in the newspapers all up and down the East Coast that July. In our neighborhood, at the supermarket, at the filling station, we were briefly famous. Nobody would take our money. The front hallway was lined with flowers. Strangers mowed the lawn and picked up our dry cleaning.

Then something else happened. It may have been the McDonald's massacre, or the Democratic convention where Mondale was nominated. It was the summer of 1984: the world was full of unexpected calamities. Mercifully, we were forgotten. The film footage of my life, which records this event in the glare and jagged shadows of midsummer, dims, grows grainy, goes dark.

I can offer only commonplaces.

A certain stony afternoon light in the sky outside my office window. The aftertaste of a thousand watery cups of coffee. My hands and feet were always cold; I wore gloves and wool socks in May. At night I turned on every light in the house: I hated the look of a shadowy corner.

Wherever I was alone, in the car, on the Metro, in my study, I had to have music playing. I went out and bought a Sony Walkman expressly for this purpose. Rossini, Stravinsky, Gounod, Telemann: it didn't matter. At work my secretary slid papers under my elbow with little notes attached: *Sign here. This is due next Monday. Call Evans at the GAO.* It was as if, by degrees, without noticing, I'd become deaf, and everyone around me was too polite to point it out.

In those days—before I took early retirement, did some desultory computer consulting, and finally stopped working for good, in 2002—I ran the small in-house publishing office at the National Security Agency. This was an administrative post, and I was a civilian, not an agent. Nonetheless, for obvious reasons, I had a very high security clearance. All twelve of us did: copyeditors, designers, secretaries, technicians. A jammed page pulled out of a Xerox machine in that office might be worth a hundred thousand dollars. I published our most sensitive materials: the reports that went to the Joint Chiefs of Staff. No one else was allowed to see them. I stood in front of the printer myself, and carried them in a plain manila envelope to the rear entrance of the Old Executive Office Building.

On the rare occasions when someone asks about my career, I offer a standard, canned response: I have nothing to add to the historical record. I suppose this makes me look like the proverbial cog in the wheel, the faceless bureaucrat. (I should know: Rachel and I were German majors in college; we read *Der Prozess* in the same seminar.) But I have to accept that silent, almost imperceptible, humiliation, because the more unpleasant truth is that I paid very little attention to the content of the materials we published. I had trouble remembering specifics even from day to day. It wasn't necessary, and it would have been distracting. I was an editor, a proofreader. Innocent people, civilians, can die, *have* died, over a misplaced comma in a sensitive document, let alone a badly chosen word, like *friendly* or *unfortunate*. In intelligence you come to appreciate that behind every word on a sheet of paper is a vulnerable human body. My counterpart at the CIA once showed me a file of examples, with photographs. For years I kept a typed quotation from Wittgenstein on the bulletin board above my desk: *Whereof one cannot speak, thereof one must be silent.*

I had a therapist, of course, assigned by my doctor. At each session he tried to explain to me what stage of the grieving process I was experiencing. I couldn't help myself: I kept insisting that he give me an exact definition of each word he used, what function it served, what could be considered X and not Y. This last point particularly bothered me. If I had a bad day at work, and missed my stop, and then barked at the cab driver for running a red light and refused to tip him, was that grief? If I found myself unexpectedly tearing up during the final scene of *Un Ballo en Maschera*, having to grope in Rachel's handbag for a tissue, was that, too, grief? And why should I victimize myself by reliving these feelings, by groping to find equivalents for them in words? Wasn't it enough to have had the feelings in the first place?

The advantage of this calamity, I told him, was that it was utterly arbitrary: a clean break, a window opened and closed. There was no way Rachel or I could blame ourselves, no way we could associate ourselves with it at all. Jolie had existed and one day had ceased to exist. We had no interest in lawsuits or safety campaigns or any of the other desiderata of grieving parents. Our mourning, I said, was purely and simply that. A clean wound. One day it would be healed.

He said he found it interesting that I thought the same rules that applied to everyone else wouldn't apply to me.

I lost my temper. I told him I thought it was a sham, these systems, these lists, these processes he kept proposing. An emotion, I said, isn't an abstraction, isn't an object, can't be verified, and therefore can't be categorized. I told him he should stop playing God.

He laughed, and said I should read Wittgenstein. That was the end of therapy for me.

Of Rachel during all that time I have only one memory: perched on the edge of Alex's bed, still in her librarian's brown mules, drying her hands on a towel, and telling a story, whispering it, into the darkened room where both children slept. Whether she made the stories up beforehand or improvised on the spot I have no idea, but she spoke without hesitation, without a text, for half an hour or forty-five minutes at a time. One day it was a romance between two hedgehogs in Scotland and the next a unicorn searching for her mother in the Himalayas. It was her unshakeable confidence in the happy outcomes of her stories, I like to think, that saved Alex and Merrill some of the pain of the randomness of this one.

In my own way, I too was an undistracted parent. I could wait an hour in the pickup line at school, or sit through a Parents' Association meeting, or spend an entire morning at a swim meet, without once checking my watch, without wishing I had brought the paper. Reagan was re-elected. It was hard to summon up the expected outrage.

I should say—by way of disclaimer? Of apology?—that I've never held particularly strong political beliefs. In this I take after my father, the postmaster of Sheffield, Connecticut, who sometimes would come out onto the post office floor and collect mail from waiting customers just for the pleasure of canceling it at his desk by hand. I shared with him a special appreciation for the beauty of the impersonal gesture. An old woman in Topeka receives her Social Security check every month not because anyone loves her or even remembers her name. The crossing guard stopping traffic in front of the elementary school need not recognize a single child that scampers past. One's human inadequacies are not the point. Efficiency, permanence, and careful design, I would have said, are the basis of real human charity and kindness.

If it was grief that I was feeling—and I still hate to use the word—it was this sense of the implacable nature of these structures that I wrapped around myself, like a blanket, or a cocoon. The momentary life of sensations, feelings, opinions, went right through me. Just existing, for the time being, was enough. I paid the mortgage, I bought groceries, I balanced the checkbook. I slept deeply and dreamlessly in the arms of a beautiful machine. It was a not entirely unpleasant existence.

In November of 1985, during an early cold snap, a homeless man named Jevon Morris froze to death on a grate downtown, in front of the National Archives. He stayed there, frozen, through the morning rush hour, with hundreds passing by on their way to work or to the Mall and the museums. They walked past a heap of rags, a motionless form wrapped in an oily blanket, unable to tell whether it—he, she—was alive or dead. Finally, around noon, the smell of putrefaction was so strong that a passing policeman noticed it.

I read the story in the newspaper sitting at our kitchen table after work, drinking tea, listening to WGMS. It was Rachel's day to pick up the children. When I finished I found I couldn't lift my arms from the table. I sat paralyzed, my elbows resting on the outspread paper, my eyes locked on the windowsill, where, I noticed, someone or something had knocked a knuckle-sized crater in the wood. The sill jutted out a few inches from the wall; it had an old-fashioned fleur-de-lis carved molding underneath, and had been painted over probably twenty times in the sixty years of the house's life, so that the original edges and fine detail had long since disappeared. I myself had applied the most recent coat, seven years before. Whatever it was had been sharp enough to dig through that quarter-inch skin of paint and gouge into the bare wood, leaving a few tiny splinters sticking out. It was, in all likelihood, Alex's fault. He sat nearest the windowsill at dinnertime, and he was the kind of careless child who wasn't above putting his soccer cleats on in the front hall, or idly swinging something hard and heavy—a pair of scissors, say—enough to chip paint, or break glass.

The radio, at that moment, was playing the opening of Charles Ives's first string quartet, *andante con moto*, with its odd, stately movement between two contrasting Protestant church-songs, as if Ives was flipping the pages of a hymnal back and forth. The music's inability to focus seemed to mock me. As I stared at it, that little divot of raw wood grew larger and larger, that I could look into it and through it, that I might be swallowed up inside it, and that in there, from the other side, came screams of ceaseless pain. Without seeing it, precisely, I knew what was there: a human face, a black man's face, pressed up against the other side of the wall, not three feet away from my own. And behind him were other faces, other bodies, packed in tight. In the space between the interior latex paint of that wall and the cedar shingles outside, I felt certain, were countless bodies, unable to move.

I know it sounds absurd. In my entire life, my thoroughly ordinary existence in a leafy, mostly peaceful, sheltered corner of the planet, I've never again experienced anything like it. If I were given to hyperbole I might say that I had looked through a window into the world's wounded soul.

I came out of the daydream, went to the sink, poured out

my tea, and quickly took a swig of Rachel's double-strength coffee, cold, straight from the carafe. The sudden shock of the caffeine would do it, I thought, would wake me up, finally, from the months of stupor, from my collapsing will, now turning into midday hallucinations, bizarre narcissistic fantasies. Either this, I thought, or a doctor for real, a psychiatrist, someone with a prescription pad and admitting privileges.

That didn't happen. Instead, almost unwillingly, I began to think about procedures, systems, chains of command. Whose job it was, for example, to write the rules that dictated to the Capitol Police when they should and should not patrol the streets for the sleeping homeless. I never doubted that there *was* such a policy. We are extremely good at writing policies in this city. And we are also good at understanding the difference between an empty rule and an enforceable one.

The radio announcer that day had a strange sense of humor. Immediately after the Ives came the Eugene Ormandy recording of Bach's "Sheep May Safely Graze," its treacly melody like a jingle from an old commercial. Ordinarily I would have risen and turned it off. But the chiming chords had the strangest, most inexplicable effect on me. I began to think of his childhood, of Jevon Morris's childhood. I saw him in his kindergarten class, on a threadbare carpet, kneeling, separate from the others. The teacher, I knew, had just shouted at him, had humiliated him, for something he hadn't done. Someone had wadded up a little ball of white bread and thrown it at him, and it was still there, stuck to his collar. He was blushing fiercely, even to the tips of his ears, and throttling back a sob.

As the music shifted into minor chords I found my eyes pooling with tears.

Someone is responsible, I thought. Someone knows why this has happened, and I will punish him.

On Wednesday of the week before Thanksgiving I took our office's box of donated canned goods to a shelter inside an abandoned school on P Street. It was all very organized; a girl not much older than Merrill took the box and started systematically unpacking it, putting each can and box into a different marked bin, one for each food group. I stared at her for a moment, at the extraordinary quickness of her slim, pale arms, and the way she methodically brushed her sandy hair out of her eyes every time she bent down. Her expressionless competence. Someone had told her that the world could be saved this way. I turned and walked up the stairs, past the sign marked *Paid Shelter Staff Only*, and knocked on the director's door.

Her name was Jenny Parker; she was about thirty-five, in jeans and a hooded sweatshirt and ripped sneakers. The ashtray on her desk was full. It wasn't an office, of course, but an old classroom, with chairs piled up against one wall. One of the windows had a pane missing; someone had tried to cover it with a piece of cardboard and Scotch tape, which had flapped away. The room was freezing, and Jenny Parker looked like she hadn't slept for a number of days. The circles under her eyes were as dark as bruises.

Listen, I said, I'm not here to take up your time. But I'm just wondering, as a citizen, if there's anything we can do on a bigger level. On a national level. I mean, this is an emergency.

People are dying in the streets.

I could tell, in the moment that it took her to respond, that she was trying hard to stop herself from saying something derisive, that it took an effort for her to control the muscles that wanted to twist her lips into a bleak and skeletal grin.

Well, she said, we appreciate whatever you can give us here. We need all the grassroots support we can get. Right now we can only keep the heat on in the building for twelve hours of the day. Six at night to six in the morning. I haven't been paid in a month and a half.

I can write you a check right now.

Well, fine, she said. We appreciate that. But there is a bill, actually, if you're interested. It's in the Senate right now, in committee. To introduce a line item for homeless services into the HUD budget for the first time. It's a lost cause, but you're welcome to write a letter if you like. You work for the government, don't you?

Why is it a lost cause?

Oh, she said, the secretary doesn't support it. Frank Murphy. He's your typical Republican troglodyte from Idaho. He doesn't understand why a Vietnam vet in a wheelchair, on disability for twenty years, missing all but three teeth, can't get a job. Sorry if I'm offending you.

No, I said, I'm not an appointee. Civil service for fifteen years.

Yeah. She looked at her watch and began checking things off on a clipboard. I'd bet you work out at Langley, she said. That would be my first guess.

Why do you say that?

Because of your eyes, she said, without looking up. I grew up here. I should know.

I did my research. I read the reports in *Congressional Quarterly* and the *National Journal* and the Hill newsletters. What she had said was true, broadly speaking. Murphy had used his allies in the House to cut off discussion of the line item in committee before the Democrats had had a chance to pounce on it. He'd been unsuccessful. There had been three days of hearings, a whole stream of activists and homeless people and lobbyists of all shapes and sizes. Hardly any of it made the news, of course, because it was all doomed in advance: an item never makes it into a department's budget without the Secretary's support. Humiliation, in this case, hadn't done a bit of good. The final vote on the bill had been delayed until January, a last-ditch attempt by the Democrats to put pressure on the White House over the Christmas holiday. Politically speaking, that year, it was one lost cause among many.

Next to one article—"Homeless Abandoned A Second Time"—I found a small, grainy photograph: a middle-aged, fair-haired man, with a long jaw and a pronounced V-shaped wrinkle in his forehead—a perpetually pained look, a man who hated to have his picture taken. He had made a small fortune consolidating stockyards; he'd chaired the Idaho Chamber of Commerce and the state GOP. There was more, but I brought out my nail scissors and cut out the picture, leaving the rest in the wastebasket. Fearing the newsprint would rub off, I slid it carefully into a nylon holder in my wallet, next to my library card, just opposite a family picture, taken in our backyard the week after Jolie was born.

The gun came from Tim's Hunting Supply, far out on Rock-
ville Pike, near Gaithersburg. It was a .38 Police Special, and
it cost $150, including the Maryland registration and license.
I used a false address in Bethesda I'd gotten out of the phone
book. When I told the man behind the counter I'd never fired
a pistol before, hoping he would at least show me how to load
it, he shook his head and handed me a gun safety pamphlet.

On my way back into the District I pulled off Georgia Avenue into a disused parking lot behind a dry cleaners and took
the pistol out of its box. In the store, on a flannel mat on the
counter beside three other guns, it had seemed small, thin-
barrelled, pedestrian. A sensible starter gun, the man had said,
you can get the ammo anywhere, it's foolproof, never jams. He
looked like he wished he had somewhere else to be.

In my hand, now, it felt heavy enough to pull my hand to
the floor.

Am I capable of this, I wondered, am I capable of murder?
A month had elapsed, now, since Jevon Morris's death. It was
early December; the children had two weeks left until winter
vacation. The next weekend we would caravan out to Turkey
Run Farm with two other families to pick our own Christmas trees, an old tradition by now. And I had grown used to
the memory of that afternoon, that strange vision, a gnawing
stomachache of an obligation unmet. It wouldn't let me rest.
I was afflicted with compassion, I thought. I was carrying it
around me like tuberculosis.

I wrapped my left hand around my right, holding the pistol

in a position of prayer. The longer I held it, the heavier it became, until I felt—I swear—that it could carry my whole body
with it, that it would lead me wherever it wanted.

Frank Murphy's house was a small white-brick Cape Cod on
Ellicott Street, near New Mexico Avenue and the Russian
Embassy, on the boundary of Rock Creek Park. The houses
on Ellicott are built high on the slope, high enough to look
out over the treetops across the park and see the Washington Monument and the Capitol dome. Many of them have
garages built into the hill at street level, but Murphy's, as it
happened, did not. He would park his car—or walk the long
downhill slope from the Metro—and approach the stone steps
up to his house on foot.

In December in Washington the light begins to fail at quarter of four; by four-thirty it is completely dark. I knew his face
only from photographs. In order to make sure it was him I
would have to be no more than ten feet away.

I left work as soon as I could, and parked in front of the
house next door at five after five. Rachel had promised the
children macaroni and cheese with cut-up hot dogs for dinner,
and I had promised I would bring home ice cream after the
meeting, by eight at the latest. Neapolitan ice cream, Merrill
was particular about that, a brick of it, from the High's dairy
store at Connecticut and Woodley Road.

When he approached, I thought, I would get out of the car,
walk as close as possible, shoot once, at his chest, get back into
the car and drive away. At the corner I would pause, momen-
tarily, roll down the passenger side window, and throw the gun

over the rail into the woods. That was all. If I was followed, if I was caught, I would not resist, I would not plead innocence. That was all I knew. As soon as I switched off the car an extraordinary calm descended over me; I could feel, or imagined I could feel, not just my heartbeat, but the tidal push-pull of blood traveling from my heart to the tiniest capillaries of my fingers and toes, and receding back again.

The car I drove in those years was a 1982 Toyota Tercel station wagon, dark blue, with vinyl upholstery. It was the first new car Rachel and I owned. I can describe it in intimate detail: the four-speed automatic transmission that lasted ten years, the parking brake that tended to stick on cold winter nights, the oil light blinking at random. By that December it had accumulated the dents and stains of three years' hard use in a family with young children. There was, for example, a tear in the ceiling fabric where someone had jammed a loose tent pole on a camping trip two summers back. I was in the habit of carrying coffee to work in a Thermos that once had leaked on the passenger seat, and that particular odor always lingered, no matter how many times we used shampoo and hung air fresheners off the rearview mirror. It had no cassette player, of course, and I didn't trust the radio at that hour, didn't want to hear traffic reports and news bulletins, the bustle of a city tidying up its day. So I had brought with me my Walkman, that delightful invention, and looped its headphones around my neck, so that the music would play *sotto voce*, underneath the sound of cars swishing by, doors slamming, leather soles clacking on the sidewalk. The cassette I had selected—need I even say this? should I have to explain everything?—was the

Eroica Symphony, Leonard Bernstein conducting.

At quarter of seven I heard the unmistakable chugging of a car downshifting, and the white glare of headlights came up over my shoulders and raked across the dashboard. A tan Mercury sedan slowed three car lengths ahead of me, and backed, at a creep, into an open spot. The driver had to correct his turn twice; even so, he left the rear of the car sticking out six inches too far from the curb, at an almost insouciant angle.

I disentangled the headphones from my neck and opened the door as quietly as I could. The gun was in my right hand. I had on a pair of thin green cotton gloves, and as I moved out into the cold I realized sweat had soaked through the palms and fingers. It was as if I'd dipped my hands in ice water. Instinctively I shoved the gun into the waistband of my pants and dug my hands into the pockets of my jacket, balling them into fists. I was afraid they might become numb.

It shouldn't have surprised me, that the man who stood up out of his car looked quite different from his photograph. He had gained weight, recently; his jacket flapped open on either side of his belly, too tight to button, and his pants looked as if they had been cinched at the waist. As he came up the sidewalk he transferred his briefcase from one hand to the other and ran his fingers through his hair, which was badly, unmistakably dyed, several shades darker than his natural color.

I've spent my life surrounded by federal bureaucrats and the unlucky outsiders, the appointees, who oversee them. I've seen the former executives dashing around with charts and graphs, with turquoise bracelets and onyx pinky rings; the buzzcut ex-Marines who want to take you out for barbeque and Jack and Cokes, the holy-eyed Mormons with the crates of Pepsi and the LDS Christmas cards. Over time—if they last long enough—all of them are defeated by Washington. They exchange their monogrammed briefcases for navy-blue duffel bags; they enroll in wine-tasting classes and buy subscriptions to the Kennedy Center. They learn the unhurried pace of their secretaries, and the names of all the security guards and the janitors. Their faces take on a certain placid softness that is easy to confuse with mere slack disappointment.

Never have I seen one as undone as Frank Murphy. Whatever pallid and insubstantial comforts he took from the world in his former life were now gone. He walked with a slight rolling motion, from side to side, as if buffeted by winds only he could feel. Everything about him seemed to express a certain muted panic, a wild grasping for reassurance.

I wouldn't call it pity, this feeling I had. Pity is far too weak a word. I was gripped with a terrible feeling that this stranger, this contemptible specimen, was someone I had known all my life. I was enmeshed; I was caught. But I had already stood up out of the car, and he could see me; it was too late to drive away. I had to complete the plan. I walked toward him, crossing the sidewalk at a slight angle, keeping my hands in my pockets, out of sight.

I lost my dog, I said. He ran off with his leash. It's never happened before.

He stopped walking and stared at me, holding his briefcase with both hands, protectively, at crotch level. His eyes seemed to rotate in their sockets, as if straining to establish parallax, to see me from the proper angle. His nose twitched. He gave a little ghostly cough, a whispery expulsion of breath.

Haven't seen him, he said. Sure he came up this way? He'll be in the park by now. That's what they all do. Run toward the park.

His breath stank of the kind of cheap red wine served with Triscuits and blocks of white cheese. He had been at a retirement party. I knew it immediately. It was what they served at a secretary's retirement party, alongside candied almonds and white layer cake.

You ought to yell for him, he said. Shouldn't you? What's his name?

Her name, I said. Trixie.

Trixie, he shouted, in a high, reedy, strangling voice. He clasped his briefcase between his knees and cupped his hands around his mouth. I had to join in. *Trixie*, we both shouted, and listened to the reverberations dying away, and the faint hiss of traffic on the Parkway, invisible in the dark below.

Well, keep walking, then, he said. It's the only thing to do.

He stuck out his hand. I recognized it; an instinctive gesture, a habit you pick up around politicians. Shake hands at the least opportunity. I loosened my right fist from the pocket of my jacket, where the edge of the glove had gotten stuck on something, a loose stitch, a hidden zipper. And in my clumsiness I butted the heel of my hand against the butt of the pistol, and it fell out of my waistband and clattered onto the sidewalk.

He looked down at it, slowly, and even more slowly raised his head and stared at me. His eyes had turned blood-black, like obsidian beads.

Where I come from, he said, his head weaving slightly, we don't carry one of those around unless we intend to use it.

I remembered a line of poetry, unable to place the author: *intimate as a dog's imploring glance, and yet again, forever, turned away.*

His mouth was a crumpled tissue of misery. Kill me, he was saying, and I won't tell, and no one will suspect you. Another random murder on a dark Washington street, a botched robbery, a man bleeding to death on the sidewalk steps outside his house.

I must have looked at him with something like horror, because his eyes widened, and he took a step back. Easy now, he said. No offense. Go on, pick it up. Get it out of here. They're illegal in this town, you know. You must not be from Washington.

As I stooped down I noticed one of his shoelaces was untied. I had a strange protective urge to reach out and tie it for him. Instead, saying nothing, I covered the pistol with my palm and scooped it up and into my pocket in one smooth motion, as if I'd been doing this kind of thing for years.

Go on, he said. Go find your dog. As if he'd just remembered why I was there.

I walked away from him; I turned, to be precise, and walked back to my car, in full view of my formerly intended victim. Without so much as looking back to see if his eyes followed me or if he was lurching up the steps as if I had never existed. It was eight-fifteen, I saw, as soon as I turned over the engine. I drove away feeling, for the first time, defeated, and relieved, by the world's sheer unrelenting ugliness.

It's possible, when you've been married for twenty-five or thirty years, when your children have grown up and moved away, to keep coming across the tail ends of conversations you started in a different decade, and to realize that whole areas of existence have lain dormant all that time, like seeds in an envelope. There's nothing unusual in that.

Or, to put it another way: when one becomes a parent, when you are charged with the care of tiny, shivering, vulnerable creatures—I picture them, all three of them, just out of the swimming pool, wrapped in towels, shuddering, their fatless bodies unable to protect them from the faintest breeze—you lose the capacity to see beyond the immediate visible world. Losing a child, of course, only makes this worse. Abstractions, including the abstraction which is romantic love, lose their lustre. You and your spouse become more like partners in a business enterprise. I'm trafficking here in pure clichés, of course. But one can't avoid them. I accepted that long ago. We are who we are.

Rachel's career and mine have had opposite trajectories. When I was at the NSA she toiled away for years as an art librarian in the city system; once Alex and Merrill went to college she returned to school and finished her PhD on Klimt and Schiele at Johns Hopkins. Now she's much in demand as a museum consultant, a specialist in securing government funding for immense and unpopular projects. A few years ago we tore down the wall between Alex and Merrill's old bedrooms and replaced the windows with a glass curtain wall, and now half the second floor is her office: a beautiful room, if I may say so, a sunlit gallery with floor-to-ceiling white bookshelves, antique barnwood flooring, and a replica George Nakashima desk. I think I enjoy it more than she does. I go in there to dust and vacuum and stare through the window through the branches of the enormous white oak that dominates our back-yard.

Last Wednesday—the fourteenth of October, 2004—she called me from a hotel in Berlin. They have her there for three weeks, helping to prepare plans for the Unification Museum. It was midnight in central Europe; five o'clock in the evening on the East Coast.

I was walking through the Alexanderplatz, she said, after the meeting, full of coffee and pastry, and I was headed back to the hotel, wrapped up in my gray wool cape, you know the one I mean, and I felt very *European*. Jürgen and Peter and the rest of them were so quiet and respectful, they complimented me on my German, they wanted to know if I was being prop-erly cared for, if I had a ride to the airport. I was floating on a cloud of gentleness and propriety. I was halfway across the square, and then, apropos of nothing, I thought, *Sobibor*. And I burst into tears. There were people all around me, but they were too polite to notice. Maybe it happens all the time here. Maybe Berliners are used to seeing strangers sobbing on streetcorners.

And then I got back to the hotel, she said, and I cleaned my-self up. I was brave about it. Peter picked me up at seven and took me to an Indian restaurant, somewhere out in the sub-urbs. It was quite a drive. He didn't say much while we were in the car. Maybe he sensed that something had happened.

Well? *Had* something happened?

I don't know, she said. Yes. I mean, I began thinking, I'm too old for this shit. I wondered whether I took too many of those new blood pressure pills. But it's not that. I just felt that—I just didn't understand how they do it, how they can look around and not feel everything just *steeped* in blood. I know, I know. It's melodramatic. And hypocritical.

Don't be so hard on yourself, I said. Things like that happen when you're traveling.

Well, she said, I was an idiot, I was feeling fragile, I don't know, but I brought it up at the restaurant. Talk about tactless and crude. I've never seen such a long silence, I think, at a dinner table. Everybody got very interested in their food.

And then finally Jürgen said to me: Let me tell you a little story.

She was quiet for long enough that I noticed a faint fizzing over the phone line, like a can of soda just opened: the only indication that she was not next door, but five thousand miles away. My heart quaked.

And? What was the story?

Give me a minute, she said. I have to stretch out my legs. I don't want to paraphrase. All right. You ready? This is what he said.

When I was young, he said, I would go to visit my grandparents in Koblenz, in the Rhine Gorge. They lived a little way outside of town on a large property that originally belonged to my great-grandfather. On one side of the property was the main house, where they stayed, and around the other side, there was a large pond, and then a little stucco house on the opposite side of that. In that stucco house lived my uncle Willem. He was blind in one eye, and he was very fat, and he lived alone, never leaving the grounds. He mowed the lawns and collected apples from the apple trees and so on. And he loved to see me whenever I would come. He loved chocolate bars, and I always brought him a whole box of them. My parents gave me the money. I was the only person in the family he would talk to.

She let out a long sigh, cracked the seal on a bottle of water, and took a swig; I heard, or imagined I could hear, the plastic knocking against her teeth. It was then, strangely, with that sound, that I understood what she was doing: relaxing into the role, into the extemperaneous pleasures of the story. She had never needed notes, only an audience. An occasion.

I don't remember when I realized that he had been in the Waffen SS, that he had been a *Lagerkommandant* at Treblinka. He certainly didn't keep it a secret. He had his uniform hanging up in a closet in his house, covered with medals. But I remember very clearly that there was a year when I fully came to realize what that meant. I watched a program, in English class, as it happens, a documentary on the Nuremberg trials. And then I had to go back to my grandparents' house the next summer and decide what I was going to do about Uncle Willem.

Would I still talk to him? Would I visit him, as I had before, and drink the very sweet cider that he made himself, in barrels, in the back of his house? Should I punish him by having nothing to do with him, like the rest of the family? I thought for a time that I should push him into the pond and make it look like an accident.

And what happened? I asked her. What did he say?

He died. He had a heart attack, that same year, in the springtime. And this is what Jürgen said: I've never in my life felt more relieved. For once in my life I was spared having to stand in judgment over what no single human being can judge. I sometimes wonder, he said, what it would be like to have no one in my own family whose crimes I could point to. I imagine it must be being in a balloon with no ballast, nothing tethering me to the earth. My own children, of course, are in that position. Their grandparents are all long dead. It's a terrible thing, to think of yourself always as innocent. Because you see the world, as it were, from the air. You can't help it. There are the innocent like you, and then there are the others, the terribly, terribly guilty.

It's late, I said. You ought to get some rest. It's another long day for you tomorrow, and then you have to catch an early flight the next morning. Christ, you're not thirty-five anymore, Rachel. Get to bed. He's a stranger. And a self-righteous jerk, if I may say so. He doesn't know anything about our lives.

Well, I started it, she said. I opened my stupid mouth. And he was polite enough not to mention any more *recent* events. Abu Ghraib. Guantánamo. I would say he showed remarkable restraint. And of course I never told him what *you* used to do for a living.

I had just opened the freezer, holding the phone in my left hand, wondering what I would eat for dinner that night. I stayed there, staring at a stack of Lean Cuisine entrees, in a cloud of cold mist. It isn't like me to get angry at her over the phone. When we argue, it's face to face, over some minor irritant: who lost the water bill? Who threw away the grapefruit spoons? But lately, I've noticed, when she's tired, sleepy, or drunk, Rachel has a glib and reckless way of running down our lives. I don't know what it's about. I ought to be more solicitous, more concerned; instead I grow annoyed and dismissive. It's as if I've decided the era of discussions in our marriage is over. Wittgenstein, I thought, Wittgenstein, you have cursed me, with the crutch of principled silence.

Oh, come on, she said. You were up to your ears in it. El Salvador, Nicaragua, Angola. Just because we never really discussed it, does that make me an idiot? Listen, I'm not excusing myself. We all lived off that salary. I could have taken the kids and left. I enjoyed it a little. It was like being married to a secret agent without the risk.

You're still drunk, I said. Go to sleep, Rachel. Before you say something really stupid.

Innocent people commit the most terrible crimes, she said. Sometimes without even lifting a finger. Don't say you don't know what I mean. You know exactly what I mean.

Not for the first time it occurred to me, remembering Frank Murphy's swollen face, the desperate thrust of his outstretched hand, that if one more streetlight had been broken on Ellicott Street I might still be in prison. But given the right circumstances, I thought, in those same months, I could have done almost anything. Set off a car bomb. Worn a dynamite belt. I had been, in my own small way, a fanatic. Listening to her, I observed this about myself with a certain perverse satisfaction. It was the one aspect of my life that had evaded all suspicion.

Oh, Rachel, I said, with a half-pantomimed sigh, as if gath-

ering up breath for some unspecified future purpose. You have
no idea. It could have been much worse.

You mean it *is* much worse, she said. She had gotten into
bed; I could see her, kicking off her shoes, lying back with the
receiver tilted up in the air. Worse than the Age of Reagan, I
mean. Who would have thought that was only the beginning?
But eventually you would have resigned. I know you would
have. Like Stu Rushfield and Parker and Bill Thorndike at the
State Department. You would have made me proud.

Maybe I would have, in one way or another, I said. But I
didn't, is that right? Isn't that what matters? I disappointed
you.

No, she said. That's the worst of it. You're a good man. You
stayed. You took care of us. At the time I don't think I would
have minded if you were Eichmann. It breaks my heart, thinking back on it. I would have overlooked almost anything. I
hope you don't mind my saying this. You can't argue with the
truth, I suppose.

It occurred to me that this would be the moment to test her
theory. A confession, if ever, was in order right then. But there
was no way I was prepared to make one. It was too late in
the day; I had already stuck a frozen pizza in the toaster oven
and poured a half-measure of Dewars over ice. I wasn't in
the mood for a marathon phone call, as if we were two teenagers. This was the converse of history, I thought, the secret
unwritten history, of men yawning late at night, too ashamed
to tell their wives who said what about the nuclear test or the
planned assasination of the prime minister, and dying of a
stroke the next day.

And yet otherwise I didn't deserve her forgiveness, or her love.

What I had been arguing for, silently, hoping for, *working* for, was to become a ghost, to disappear, like the others, into the walls of my own house. I didn't want to replicated. I never wanted there to be another story like this one. If I could, I thought, I would stop this story, too. If it were a tape recorder, I would go back to the beginning and erase it, erase the sound of my own voice. The weight of years on these sagging vocal cords, the gravelly burr, the pretend wisdom. No one should be allowed to speak this way, I thought, even into the unknown, even to you. But I drank the drug of inertia long ago. I can't spit it out.

No, I said. You can't argue with the truth.

In our living room we have a framed photograph I took of Jolie at six, playing in the sprinkler in the backyard. She looks over her shoulder at the camera, her face crinkled up with pleasure, the water striking between her shoulder blades and spraying everywhere, dotting the lens with droplets.

She had enormous bottle-green eyes and very dark, very straight brown hair. And a dimpled chin, and fair skin, much paler than any of the rest of us. My mother was descended from an Anglo-Irish family, and I suppose a few of those genes made their way to her. She sunburned easily and freckled everywhere. A little slip of a girl, my God. Even by that summer she was just four feet tall.

Schafe können sicher weiden,
Sheep can safely graze
Wo ein guter Hirte wacht.
where a good shepherd watches over them.
Wo Regenten wohl regieren,
Where rulers are ruling well,
Kann man Ruh und Friede spüren
we may feel peace and rest
Und was Länder glücklich macht
and what makes countries happy.

At the kitchen table, I cut the brown paper backing with a razor blade, remove the paperboard and the photograph and the mat, and carefully lift out the square pane of glass, so no one will be injured; the glass goes into the recycling bin, and the rest of it into a garbage bag, which I wrap around again and again, like a precious parcel, and carry out to the sidewalk for tomorrow's pickup. I cut the brown paper backing with a razor blade; I expect it to hurt; I expect it to bleed. I expect the razor blade to stray across the palm of my outstretched hand. But that is never the way it is with me. In my life I have been the shepherd watching from the air, praying, don't look up, don't let me see your faces, for who knows what I'll do to the world if I lose you.

Lives of the Saints

I t's because you're a woman that you don't want me to die, Tayari says.

On their way home, the 6 train sidling its slow way through the South Bronx, she has her head in his lap, her long gangly legs splayed out over three seats, fingers hooked into his dreadlocks. She likes to feel them brushing her face: to take the cowrie shells between her teeth and threaten to crack them like sunflower seeds. By habit or dramatic instinct he speaks without looking at her, staring down his smoky reflection in the opposite window as it flickers in and out of view, as if hypnotized by the repetition: so many intermittent identical versions of himself.

Fuck you, she says.

No, I'm serious. There's a whole theory that explains it. Women and men perfectly complement each other. Numerologically. It's the ideal balance of energies. The difference between prime numbers and all the other numbers.

She nestles her cheek against his sweatshirt and feels the packages crackling underneath. I'm dating the Scarecrow, she thinks: all rustle, no heart. Or was it the Tin Man with the heart, and the Scarecrow with the brain? She could never keep them separate, those two inanimates.

Listen, she says, you got the kind for heavy flow, right?

Baby. It's not shopping, it's *stealing.*

Last time you were pissed when I got regular M&M's instead of peanut butter.

He gives her a look, as if to say, don't tell *me* what matters.

There's this expert, he says, Adid, teaches at CUNY? He says that certain men are like prime numbers. They're these unique, indivisible presences in the universe. They can only do one thing well, they're geniuses at that one thing, but useless at everything else. But women, on the other hand, are inherently divisible, multiplicable. They, like, *surround* men with support and energy. Shit's just common sense if you ask me.

In the cold glare of the train compartment, which turns a clean white t-shirt the color of pit stains, his skin looks downright grey, like an old sidewalk. It amazes her that people don't stop and stare. One of these days, she's going to have to ask him how he turned that color. If only for the historical record.

She reaches up and runs her fingers over the line of Sanskrit tattooed at the base of his neck. You're right, she says. I don't want you to die. No one should have to die for their art. I want to grow old with you, she might say, just to twit him, to see how he'd respond. She knows he has a soft romantic side, like a cat's belly; but woe to the one who scratches it, unmindful of the slashing claws! Like the Ché poster he has tacked up on the bathroom door: *At the risk of seeming ridiculous, I remind you that all revolutionaries are guided by great feelings of love.*

Or else you're just like *them*, he snaps, as if reading her mind, and gestures with his chin down the car. A tiny girl stares back at them, bunching the hem of her mother's skirt in her fist. Her hair a mass of pencil-thin cornrows at crazy, Medusa-snake angles, each one neatly tagged with a pink barrette. With her free hand she holds out a toy cell phone by its antenna, as if to say: you look lost, want to make a call?

Oh, come on, she says. Reproduction is righteous. The cycle of life. Isn't that what you always say?

He breaks away from his reflection and stares down at her, his eyes ice-blue, like little novelty lightbulbs. Baby, he says, his voice bright with affection and pity, you can think whatever you want. But we're not into cycles. We're into straight fucking lines.

His apartment-not-an-apartment takes up the whole southeast side of the abandoned U-Store-It in Hunts Point: a vast, concrete-floored hangar divided in two by a molded plastic wall meant to simulate exposed brick, a fly-by-night speculator's fantasy of a loft condo, long since gone belly-up. There's the little room where they sleep, on a bed stead he built of boards and cinderblocks, with the microwave that never works and the hotplate that works okay, and the big room, for his projects, for the videos, festooned with cables and lights and disassembled computers, scramblers, sequencers, mixing consoles. And props: green banners with white Arabic script, photographic backdrops of buses exploding and the Twin Towers falling, an orange New York State Prisons jumpsuit he scored from an ex-con in Mott Haven, a bullet belt from a surplus store, a machete, various plastic and metal prop guns, and real ones, too, tilted against chairs and piled on tables like toys in a nightmarish playroom.

He chose the location, he says, because it's across the street from Real Azteca, *lo mejor comida Oaxaqueña en NYC,* and he loves tamales and doesn't cook. The electricity's stolen, the water's stolen, the TV powered by a concatenation of handmade satellites spread across the roof; the rent, seven hundred in twenties in a paper sack, goes to Grigory and Yevgeny, brothers with puffy, collapsed faces like rotting Jack-o'-lanterns, who show up the first of every month in a Buick Regal with tinted windows and no rear license plate.

But since there's no Duane Reade or CVS or proper supermarket for twenty blocks in any direction, and because, in the end, she's a child of the suburbs, they do their shoplifting in Midtown at rush hour. In the long flickering aisles, ignored by the security waif fiddling his walkie-talkie at the entrance, they shovel loot into backpacks, duffel bags, under oversized sweaters, even packing it into Tayari's Rasta hat. There are the cameras, sure, but who's watching them, Sarita from Bangalore fifteen-deep in customers up front?

The fruit of righteousness, Tayari calls whatever they steal. *Prasadam,* holy food.

That's how they met, back when he thought it was still safe to move around in daylight, in familiar neighborhoods. She was a Halloween temp at Galaxy Props Costumes and Magic on Broadway and 11th, her third semester, and he wandered in and asked about cloth markers, their reflective properties and tendencies to fade under bright light. It was charming, the way

he assumed she actually knew things. Underneath the double
eyebrow spikes and the plastic clips threaded through the tops
of his ears he had a twelve-year-old's guileless face, a face that
collected information for its own sake, a wholly uninformed
and wondrous appreciation for the world. She'd been reading
Gramsci and thinking about revolution, which in Maplewood
was a ridiculous thing to do, a pimply suburban cliché, but
here in the world of dull-lit classrooms and earnest young pro-
fessors with unironic scarves and wet thrift-store boots drying
on the radiator, it was real, it was serious, shit, it was *happening*,
all the signs were pointing that way, Seattle, the WTO, not
to mention the unmentionable, that—which—happened—
twenty—blocks—away, and Tayari walked into her store looking exactly like the future: festooned with cartridge belts and
covered with bulging pockets, tattooed with symbols of some
private mythology, and covered in dust the color of ashes and
powdered concrete, a walking headstone, a dead baby in plain
sight. She watched him pacing the aisles back and forth, palm-
ing brushes and jars of glitter, tubes of superglue and latex
cement, and when he walked out he tossed a greasy piece of
cardboard with a scrawled email address onto her counter,
and said, *prasadam,* and he had no idea what it meant, and she
felt the floor of her stomach giving way.

He makes martyr videos, she told her mother, the last time
they saw each other, at Joe's Coffee on Waverly, before a thick
velvet curtain of silence fell between them, as if to say, *End of
Act One,* and she stopped buying minutes for her cell phone.
Not that he believes in martyrdom per se. He's interested in

the semiotics of the form, the performance of violence in virtual space. It was all crap she'd lifted straight from her Media Studies T.A., the short bald one with the square black glasses she always tried to impress. It's very challenging stuff, she said, no doubt, but that's what the art world's all about these days. The concept *is* the execution. The era of the art object is behind us. You have to be there. But you can't, because of technology, because it's happening everywhere at once. That's what he's trying to do, you know, challenge the viewer. *Indict* the viewer. *Assault* the viewer.

That doesn't sound like art, her mother said, so infuriatingly literal. That sounds like a prison sentence. I don't like it. I think it's self-destructive and decadent and asinine.

Well, you would. Of course you would.

Listen, her mother said. And I don't want you to take this the wrong way. Give me a sense of his background.

Meaning is he black?

Well? *Tayari?*

If you assume you make an ass out of u and me, she said, triumphantly. He's non-ethnically identified. He's against genetic descriptions. I don't even know what he is, honest. He may have had plastic surgery. We don't talk about it. I respect his privacy.

She doesn't tell her mother that his previous project, the one he's famous for, involved three hundred and sixty-five home preganancy tests he'd peed on, one every day for a year, and stapled to a board. *False Positive*, it was called. There were three pink plus signs, one in June and two in November. It was in a group show at Maurice Espa and all the articles, even the one in the *Times*, mentioned him. She doesn't tell her how it feels to go to *the* opening of *the* show hand-in-hand with *the* Boy Of The Moment, the art-school girls shooting her envious dirty looks, running down her vintage 1996 Anna Sui skirt with the weird fringe. She doesn't tell her how it feels to meet Michael Musto and Julian Schnabel and Diane Von Furstenberg and Salman Rushdie, all in the same room, all at once, and run across Ninth Avenue to score coke at the Gansevoort Hotel, how it feels to drive up the FDR at 6 a.m. puking out the cab window. She doesn't say, wishes she could say, it's like discovering that a day is actually twenty-five hours long, and all but that one extra hour is wasted.

He's learning Tamil, she wants to tell her. He goes to classes in Jackson Heights. After that, Arabic. Then New Testament Greek. He wants to go to Gaza. He gets three thousand channels of satellite TV and has six months of Al Jazeera saved on his hard drives. He has a real Kalashnikov, the original Czech model, bought on eBay, of course. With a double banana clip. He owns *detonators*. If the government knew we would both be in prison. They'd think it meant something.

Listen, he said one time, when they were perched in their usual spot, eating tamales rolled in foil, seated on milk crates, with a view of the whole intersection. If you want my philosophy in a nutshell, here it is. We're consumers of politics as much as, say, movies or soft drinks or shoes. All these causes, you know, prefab, you can shop for them, you know, like at college orientation? With all the tables? Human rights this and women's that, Darfur, genital mutilation, global fucking warming,

PETA? And I'm just, like, take it to the next level.

Because it's not like the suffering isn't real.

Yeah, okay, but what exactly do you mean, *real?* I mean, we need to take that concept seriously. I mean *real* as in you can touch it, you can taste it. Not this Matrix crap, you know, computer-generated, postmodern, is he or isn't he, these parlor games. Real means it *hurts*. Real meaning it collapses all distinctions. Real reduces the world to *pain*.

He took a fingerful of salsa verde on the tip of his pinky and snorted it in a quick, offhand gesture. Whew! he screamed, and a crowd of seagulls feasting on tortilla scraps erupted in a cloud of beating wings into the sky.

You're an idiot, she said. Don't show off. Look, you made them stop their soccer game.

No importa, he shouted, waving across the avenue at the five Guatemalan men who had paused, one holding the ball cocked beneath his heel, staring back at them. *No se preocupa. Esto es mi problema solamente.*

Crazy fucking white boy, she heard, or thought she heard, one of them saying to the others, over the screaming of the gulls and revving of a passing motorcycle.

Seriously, he said, I made a promise to myself, a long time ago. Before any of this shit happened to me. Before I went to art school.

I didn't know you went to art school.

Of course I went to art school. That's the keys to the fucking kingdom, you know that. You have to get stamped and sent out, readymade. With the right logo you can sell anything. But I'm talking about ages before that, when I was still living in

Detroit, in the Cobra Negra squat, doing graffiti.

You never told me any of this.

Well, I'm telling you now, he said. I lost an armwrestling contest with this crackhead former wrestler, the Bandit, and the motherfuckers made me move to the basement as punishment. I had a mattress half chewed out by mice and had to use rubber sheets, 'cause the pipes dripped hot water on me all night long. I spent three months down there. Didn't have two dollars to my name the whole time. I was dumpster diving, living with just the clothes on my back. Would have done better on out on the street. But, you know, it was still OK, because I had with me the three most beautiful books ever written. The Bible. *Das Kapital*. And Bakunin's *Catechism of a Revolutionary*. And I would get so high, you know, I was starving, I mean I was like sixteen years old and hardly eating, my system was feeding on itself, I went weeks without taking a shit. I would read with my flashlight till three, four in the morning, and then I would go walk up and down Cass Avenue, and not see a single human being for blocks, sometimes. And then one time I had this vision. You know about the penis fish?

T, she said, what the fuck are you talking about?

The penis fish, he said, *Candirú*, it's called, *Vandellia cirrhosa*. It lives only in the Amazon. Burroughs wrote about it in *Naked Lunch*. If you take a piss in the river it gets sucked up into your urethra and puts out these little barbs and feeds, just sucks the blood right out of you. It's the most painful sensation you can possibly imagine. Well, look, I'd read about it somewhere, and it just came to me all of a sudden. You enter through the pleasure organ. That's art, don't you see, disinterested aesthetic appreciation, *jouissance*, whatever you want to call it. That's how you get in, and then you put out your barbs, and you mangle the whole fucking system. You're like Skywalker shooting his missile into the heart of the Death Star. So that's what I want to do. He held up his two fingers in a Y and thrust them at her eyes. In through the eyes and bleeding out of every other goddamned orifice in thirty seconds.

What really gets me, her mother wrote to her in a letter, afterward, *it isn't the subject matter of his art, it isn't his personal hygiene or his politics or his questionable beliefs about real estate, it's you and the way you're acting, the whole Lee Krasner to Jackson Pollock attitude. It's straight out of 1950 and it terrifies me. He can only make you his muse if you let him.*

And it's true that she hasn't danced, hasn't thought about dancing, hasn't read a copy of *Dance News* or been to a concert since he gave her the lecture at Joe's in February, since he said, the only kind of dancing I'm interested in is dancing around the bonfires we'll build in the middle of Park Avenue one day, when we break up Biedermeier chairs like matchsticks and fire up the society ladies' wardrobes and throw their daughters in by the hair for good measure.

I wish you wouldn't talk that way, she said. Don't lick your lips. Do you know you do that? It's disgusting.

Promise me, he said, promise me you'll give it up, until—

Until?

Until you find a way to make it *matter*.

That's his whole thing, an aesthetic credo cobbled together from Adorno and Brecht and John Cage and Sonny Rollins, if only he would admit it. I waited, he always says, I was ready to give up art altogether, I got rid of all my old crap, would have burned it in a pile except it would have been a toxic plume and that's eco-racism. I waited until I found something that mattered. Like Sonny says. Don't come in until you have something to contribute.

In 484 the king of the Vandal tribe, Huneric, issued an edict against the Catholic Church in North Africa. In this persecution, the Catholic doctor Liberatus, his wife, and their two young sons were apprehended. Liberatus' wife was subsequently told the falsehood that Liberatus had apostatized. When afterward she was led to her trial and saw her husband standing near the spectators, she angrily grabbed him and rebuked him for denying his faith. But her husband quickly told her the truth of the matter: "In the name of Christ, I remain a Catholic." Both Liberatus and his wife were executed. Their sons were put to death by drowning, as was another seven-year-old Catholic boy, who cried out, "I am a Christian," as he was dragged away from his distraught mother.

It's one of the books he keeps on the rusting steel shelf above his desk in the studio: *Lives of the Saints*, a heavy hardbound maroon thing with gold lettering, the kind of book you give as a present, a display copy, a book for people who don't actually read. Inside the pages are thick and soft, spongy, inferior quality, and the ink rubs off, like newsprint. She started paging through it one night when he was supposed to be out doing graffiti.

Late in the afternoon of July 27, 1936, soldiers of the Popular Front raided the Dominican friary of Calanda, Spain. Seven Dominicans and a sixty-eight-year-old parish priest, Father Manuel Albert Gines, were taken by truck to an execution site outside the city. Along the way, the eight recited the rosary aloud. One of the Dominicans, Father Felicisimo Diez Gonzalez, gave a fountain pen as a present to their persecutors. Upon disembarking from the truck, each of the eight priests forgave their executioners. The priests exclaimed together, "Long live Christ the King," as they were gunned down.

She's never had much of a spiritual life herself. Not in conventional terms. His father was a boring, mainline, coffee-and-Nilla-Wafers Presbyterian; her mother's parents were Catholics, Polish Catholics, but they both died before she was born—smokers, lovers of American fast food, Arby's especially, the curly fries, the heaps of fatty sliced beef, who knew why?—and then years later her mother did some genealogical research and discovered, incredibly, that they were Jews, that they had grown up together as adopted orphans from families dead in the Holocaust. It was all there, it was documented. Which meant that she was Jewish, too.

She was fifteen at the time, and what her mother did, after spreading the books and binders and printouts across the kitchen table and explaining the whole story, how this thumbnail-sized grainy photograph connected to this scrawl on an Ellis Island ledger connected to this yellowed page from the Warsaw Ghetto archives, was ask if she wanted to see a therapist. Or a rabbi. Those were her options. I feel this is so much larger than us, her mother said. This is beyond—this is more than—and she looked genuinely lost, the lower half of her face coming in and out of focus. I mean, this is historical, she said, with an expression of awe, as if they'd been FedExed the Mona Lisa. It was disgusting, it was the first five minutes of a Lifetime movie, and she'd done the only thing a self-respecting adolescent could do: get up and walk away, pretend it never happened, that she had never been parented at all. *Chthonic*: her favorite SAT word. Born of the earth itself, born out of a toxic North Jersey flowerbed: that was as far back as she wanted the story to go.

But on the other hand, apart from her home life and its comfortable stickiness, its soccer cleats and parking-lot parties and PSAT's, there's the feeling she gets listening to certain CDs, the ones she's loved for years, the ones that stick with her. Lauryn Hill, "To Zion": in a certain mood, after a long shower when the hot water's on, it gives her the shakes.

> *Unsure of what the balance held*
> *I touched my belly, overwhelmed*
> *By what I had been chosen to perform*

It's genocide, Tayari says, genocide against the black man, against the Mexicans, against the teenagers whose fierceness to reproduce is what, in the end, they're all most afraid of. He won't have condoms around, won't steal them for her, won't wear one, though he got her some rhythm method pamphlets and found some Swedish method online that lets you enter your cycle and figure out when you'll ovulate every month for the next fifty years. In his calmest moments he admits they can't possibly do the pregnancy thing right now, not with his project at its current stage, not with the dumpster diving and stealing and living hand to pocket. The guys from Chiapas and Vayaguera and Michoacán tell him to move down there, he could run a free clinic, set up a radio station, teach Internet to the guerillas. Living is cheap, they say, you wouldn't believe it, we'll set you up with a place with your *mujer*, you can have babies, raise a garden, go back to the land, be campesinos for awhile.

But as with everything he's a little scattershot, his principles flexible, his promises fungible, everything inextricable from desire and living in the moment, and so they're not careful and don't always stick to the dates the computer spits out. He likes to do it from behind, and always swears he'll pull out in time, but there's nothing she can do if he gets carried away in the pulling and pushing, the plunging and long weepy exhalations, he's back there with hands on her hips, in the saddle, in the driver's seat. He says he feels something driving him into her, some larger force, some heavy-handed and dirty-minded deity swatting him on the back, and there's nothing he can do.

And her period's never been regular. In high school she went six months with only a little spotting and never told anyone, kept asking Mom for the monthly box of Playtex so she wouldn't freak out. Tried to eat more green vegetables, tried to get more sleep, and eventually it came back as if nothing had ever happened. A capricious and sometimes vengeful overlord, her cycle, sometimes appearing out of nowhere, ruiner of a hundred pairs of underwear and a blue peasant skirt she'd loved. So give up, she tells herself, give in, let go of predictability, that bourgeois fantasy. *The joy of my world is in Zion.* It sounds so good she half-believes it.

The thing is that one of them needs a job, for now, an untraceable, untaxable job, before *False Positive* sells. There are three collectors interested and the gallery owner is trying to play them off each other, but it's complicated, the economy's tanking, unsurprisingly, the Dow is down in the 8s, and these guys are up to their ears in it, watching every last fifteen thousand. And they all want studio visits, they want to be Tayari's best friend, suss him out, gauge his potential and his predictability. They think I'm going to flame out, T says, but the key is *when*. If I jumped in front of a bus tomorrow, no dice: not even enough for a gallery retrospective. But if I can stick it out five more years, I'll be the Basquiat of the '00s. He pronounces it *oh-oh*s, like a redundant breakfast cereal. It takes her a minute to realize what it means. The zeroes, the thousands, the decade without a name, she thinks, when I was young. The *oh-oh* generation. She's not sure she likes the sound of that.

She mentions the cashflow issue to Roger, who works at the Juvenile Justice across the avenue, but somehow gets to take long lunch breaks, squatting outside Real Azteca and eating tamales real slow, taking swigs from a two-liter of champagne cola between bites. He's got diabetes, he says, that's why he needs the extra sugar, which makes no sense to her.

Listen, girl, he says, and gives her a sideways look, a mirthful squinting grin. How far you willing to go?

What, you mean, like Staten Island or something?

Naw. I mean are you a risk-taker? Type-C personality. Willing to think outside the box.

Her heart jumps like a salmon breaching its way up a dam. If you're asking me to take my clothes off, she said, *no*. Nothing sexual.

Girl, he says, guffawing, ain't no one in this neighborhood dying to hit your skinny ass. Plus your witch-doctor boyfriend wouldn't take too kindly. Gimme your number. I got the perfect thing. Good money, all in cash. And it's close by.

What he means, it turns out, what the perfect thing is, is driving the Rikers van that leaves from 134th and Woodside, ferrying the mothers and girlfriends and babies of Mott Haven's vast prison population for weekly visits. It's a tricky, stomach-twisting ride, the Deegan Expressway over the Triboro Bridge to the Grand Central Parkway, and then the long causeway out to the island itself. Twelve riders a pop, and she makes $40 a ride, there and back.

At first she wears T's Carhartt hoodie pulled up over her head and stares straight forward, not even looking in the rearview mirror, not wanting to start any conversations she can't finish. What's a white girl doing driving the Rikers van out of the projects? She ought to give one of them the job. All she has to do is sign back up at NYU, or even the New School, even Parsons School of Design, and lo, her bank account replenishes itself, her dormitory bills are paid. I don't understand, she says to Roger, why would anyone want me, all you need for this job is a driver's license anyway.

Girl, he says, you know how much driver's ed cost? Let alone insurance, paying your tickets, taking off work to stand in line even if you get a ride to the DMV? If it was so god-damned easy what they need a Rikers van for anyhow?

So gradually she relents. It's a public service, she tells herself, someone has to do it, and the little girls, who could resist them, their hair bound up in puffy ponytails or thin silky braids, rainbows of barrettes and beads, the older ones coming right from school in navy jumpers with the matching tights, Dewanya and Taniqwa and Tiffany and Coral and Mo'netta with the apostrophe. The mothers she can take or leave—indistinct presences, thunder-thighs in tight jeans, dark-circled eyes, braying into cell phones and reaching out for the occasional slap—but the girls eye her conspiratorially and every so often lean up into the well between the front seats for a conversation in low voices.

You a teacher?

What's your name?

Is that your real color hair?

Are you Spanish or just white?

You live around here?

Who's inside, she wants to ask them, ask them all, is your daddy, your brother, your big sister, what's the sentence, what's he in for, what's your favorite color, what subject is your favorite in school besides recess? But Ray, the boss, is right there beside her riding shotgun, flipping twenties into bundles and tapping numbers into his calculator with two thumbs. His eyes dead as the brackish oil-slicked puddles on Lefferts when it rains. So all she gets are the names. Entries in the cosmic logbook: those owed some unspecified and impossible debt.

Righteous, Tayari says when she tells him, finally, knowing he'll never ask, never wondering about the fresh infusions of cash in the Hello Kitty plastic zippered envelope they keep above the drop-ceiling panels in the bathroom. I knew you'd find some way to connect, he says, kissing her on the bone behind her right ear, flicking his tongue against the lobe. It's all a part of the equation, the grounding, the here-and-now. Our work comes from the people *for* the people.

He's been reading Amiri Baraka again, the post-Beatnik, post-*Blues People*, post-LeRoi Jones Baraka, the Baraka of the Black Arts Theater and *It's Nation Time*. He's beginning to see that the videos are just a preliminary stage. The big problem is mediation, he says, everything takes place on a screen these days, it's like we think that's the only way we can communicate anymore, in pixels, but we have to get away from that, we have go *through* the pixelated vision and *into* the real, we need to get back to Artaud, the theater of cruelty, you know?

When he talks this way she feels she's floating off into the distance on little curls and eddies of nausea. A queasy river, a sickly sea. I'm sick, she starts thinking one afternoon, lies down in bed, and wakes five hours later in the dark, feeling as if she's been stapled to the mattress. She needs Tylenol, she needs chamomile tea with honey, none of which they have, none of which he would ever think of on his own. Her mouth tastes of sour milk and radishes, and the room is filled with an overwhelming funk she never noticed before, a smell of semen and sweat and lipstick, though she hasn't worn lipstick in six months.

Baby, he says, standing silhouetted in the doorway, a sexy profile, inarguably, with the dustmop hair and the slender powerful legs and the soldering iron's handle protruding from his waistband like an erect and eerily rectangular penis. We're going to Miami. You're going to be in a fashion show.

It's at Miami Basel, of course, the biggest art fair in the known world, and as the gallery guy explains it, it's one of those synergy things, all the rage these days, art-design-fashion, everyone hustling everyone else. Specifically in this case Vogue and WWD and Conde Nast and Balenciaga and Jack Spade and Mikamoto and a slew of other names that sound important and expensive, versus a crew of up-and-comers, hungry young ones with no reputation and no choice. *Give us your version of a "fashion show" in the year 2020,* the fax reads.

Love the scare quotes, she says. You really want to do this?

Oh, baby, he says, you have no idea. *I* don't want this. The *universe* wants it. Fuck, the universe *demands* it.

And when she tells him, finally, he neither explodes in rage nor dissolves in tears, blames neither her nor himself, proposes neither abortion nor adoption nor some extraordinary third option, one she can't identify, one she was secretly hoping for. In the range of possible human reactions she has no idea where to place his skeptical, hawklike expression, not wanting to call it what it is: calculating. He might even be counting under his breath. As if she's told him how much she spent doing the laundry.

Righteous, he says, his new favorite word. It's all falling into place. We're raising the stakes. We're fucking raising the stakes!

Later, when she's forty, fifty, when her children have grown and left her sitting at her own kitchen table somewhere, nursing her third cup of coffee—because she does imagine these things, does think of herself, eventually, retreating to some leafy, wholesome, low-impact kind of place, some small town in Vermont or Oregon or Nova Scotia—then and only then will she look back and be able to measure the sheer depth, the profundity, of the change, the moment she played her small part in, as earth-changing in its way as Ginsberg reading *Howl* in San Francisco in 1955, as Coltrane playing the Village Vanguard the second time, as Merce Cunningham dancing in *For John Cage*, as Sonic Youth playing CBGB in 1981. She won't remember name of the album Tayari chose, the Missing Foundation's *Destroy White Culture*. She won't remember the three hours they spent at the rented house in Palm Beach with the porn producer with the terrible skin and meth-rotted teeth, who produced one naked pregnant woman after another, with dead eyes and smiles shellacked in place, until T found the five he wanted.

But she will remember the nails, and how they had to be sterilized for an hour, how she spent an entire afternoon tonging them in and out of a stockpot, laying them out on fresh white towels like surgical instruments, which, after all, was what they were, what they had to be. While T recorded the final video on his Webcam in the next room. There were long stretches of clanging, battering music, interspersed with shouted passages from the Qu'ran, the Book of Jeremiah, the *Bhagavad Gita*, Sun-tzu. When she brought him a sandwich for lunch he was naked, with a single blue stripe painted down the center of his body, an Uzi in each hand. She smelled something burning in the room, and bent down to check the surge protectors and the outlets, feeling around the electrical tape for excess heat. That she'll remember too, the burning smell that seemed to come out of nowhere. He had a series of headbands stenciled in English and Arabic, and she remembers only one of them: *You Will Pay.*

Because it was her job to be the last on the walkway, because she had to be the one to pound the nails in, while Tayari seethed through his gag and wrenched his head away, she'll never know exactly how long it lasted until the black-helmeted policemen came racing down the aisles, and whether there was even one moment, in the end, when the whole world was his name, TAYARI ALPHA, in giant black letters, and five naked bodies, five women's bodies, their breasts comically inflated, their bellies distended, barely able to squeeze into the dynamite belts she'd lovingly sewn with full-belly panel elastic, their faces masks of glittering makeup. There will be video, but she will never watch it, not in the solitary holding cell in McCandless Prison, where she waits two weeks for her father's lawyer to negotiate bond, and not in the basement apartment of her parents' house in Maplewood, where she lives out the rest of the pregnancy sucking ginger lollipops and knitting unwearable scarves. What she remembers is the snap of the rubber gloves against her wrists, and the strange imbalance of the weight of the hammer in her right hand and the disappearing lightness of the nail in her left. Her hands did not shake; her eyes grew dry, forgetting to blink. When T felt the tip of the nail pressed into the thin skin between the tendons in his palm and pulled it instinctively, protectively, **toward his chest**, she was the one who seized it and bent it cruelly back into position according the lines spraypainted on the plywood. This is what she will remember in the hospital, her legs splayed, the baby's tiny skull splitting her in half, breathing the pain out through gritted teeth and refusing to scream: how, when she pounded the first nail in and he bellowed like a electrocuted ox, and calmly reached for the next, thinking, every suffering saint was born of a woman's pain, thinking, how much easier it would be if I could drive them into my own skin.

Acknowledgments

These stories previously appeared in different form in the following publications: "Nobody Ever Gets Lost" in *American Short Fiction* and *Drunken Boat,* "The Answer" in *Granta,* "The World in Flames" in *Witness* and *Five Chapters,* "Amritsar" in *The Atlantic Monthly,* "Sheep May Safely Graze" in *Threepenny Review, The PEN/O.Henry Awards 2010,* and *The Pushcart Prize, XXXIV: Best of the Small Presses,* "The Call of Blood" in *Harvard Review,* and "Lives of the Saints" in *Ploughshares.* I'm grateful to the editors and staff of these publications for their patience and assistance.

This book would not have been possible without the support of the Mrs. Giles Whiting Foundation, the National Endowment for the Arts, Montclair State University, and The College of New Jersey.

Thanks to Sookyoung Lee, Nadia Ellis, Stephen Russell and Hache Carrillo for their help translating Korean, Jamaican patois, and Spanish in these stories.

The poem quoted in "The Call of Blood" is from Edgar Lee Masters, *Spoon River Anthology.* "The Answer" contains an excerpt from Sayyid Qutb's *In the Shade of the Quran,* translated anonymously. "Sheep May Safely Graze" contains a line from Rilke's *Sonnets to Orpheus,* translated by Stephen Mitchell.